GHOST HILLS

H . BEDFORD-JONES

GHOST HILLS

H. BEDFORD-JONES

ALTUS PRESS • 2015

© 2015 Altus Press • First Edition—2015

EDITED AND DESIGNED BY
Matthew Moring

PUBLISHING HISTORY
"Ghost Hills" originally appeared in the July 26–August 16, 1913 issues of *The Cava-lier* magazine (Vol. 31, No. 2–Vol. 32, No. 1).

THANKS TO
Gerd Pircher

TABLE OF CONTENTS

CHAPTER I

MONTENAY'S LUCK

"**D**ONE, TAKE-A-CHANCE!"
"Huh?"

"Last letter's done, and I'm ready."

"Time you were. Been writing all afternoon. Come on."

"What are all these breeds around for this morning? Isn't that unusual this time of year? Anything doing?"

"Sure—lots. They weren't breeds, but pure-bloods. That's what I've been after you to break away for. Hold still, Rad—listen!"

The two figures paused in the shelter of the stockade, beside an ancient little cannon on its crumbling carriage near the flagstaff. Above them flared and danced the lights in uncouth streamers and bands from horizon to horizon, and around lay the clay-plastered log buildings of Fort Tenacity, silent on the snow.

Despite the huge furs that enveloped both figures, their faces stood out clear-cut against the sky, distinct in the weird shadow-light. The one was raw-boned, gaunt with the trail, strong hewed of brow and nose and mouth, for Tom Macklin, or "Take-a-chance Macklin," as he was known from the Mackenzie to the bay, was a son of the lights by breed and birth and choice.

The other was finer-featured, save for his nose, which lent the suggestion of an eagle as he leaned forward, listening. But for the eyes, his face was not distinctive. The mouth was a trifle too firmly set, perhaps; the chin a trifle too short, but the level brown eyes blazed out with a strange tensity as if the owner sought something that lay far out of ken over the horizon.

Even so had Barr Radison sought, for the better part of his life. Blessed with money, he was cursed with the ancient curse of the wanderlust. Ever had he sought the thing undreamed of—the thing that had no name, and ever had he found that beyond the far skyline lay a new horizon, empty. The two men had met in Winnipeg ten weeks before, and Radison had looked Macklin in the eye for a long moment.

"Take me north, will you?" he had asked simply.

"Sure. I'll take a chance on your looks. Stick around—something may turn up."

The "something" had turned up. It had taken them north and northeast; it had drawn them west and then north again, until finally it had brought them to Fort Tenacity. And beyond Tenacity there was nothing.

Beyond Tenacity the breed trappers were not. Beyond Tenacity were Cree and Chipewa, with red snow between. Behind Tenacity lay white snow and the trail of the packet, traveled twice a year, for where the mail comes there must be no red snow.

In the north the mail is the law, relentless, irrevocable, unbreakable. Men are little things, and the mail is the greatest thing, for so the white man has ordained. But beyond Tenacity there was none to ordain.

"Hurry up—it's blamed cold out here!" exclaimed the American after a moment. Both men were staring at a log building next the store, which gleamed dull light through its one window. It was the largest building in the post, where canoes and dogsleds were stored at other times.

"Hold on," rejoined Macklin stolidly. "Take a chance on hearing something—there he goes! Lord, what a man—stark drunk at that!"

From the building, which had a moment since echoed a raspy

fiddle-squeak, rose a single resonant, liquor-charged bass voice. It was not singing; rather, it was intoning in a most monotonous and sing-song manner, as if it had been caught unawares by the stoppage of the Red River Jig.

> … and he who will this toast deny:
> Down among the dead men,
> Down among the dead men,
> Down, down, down, down—
> Down among the dead men
>   Let him lie!

Radison grunted as the voice died out. "Pity but he'd learn the tune—it's a heap better than the words! By thunder, I'll take a shy at it just to show him how!"

Without warning he raised his voice, unheeding the quickly protesting hand of Macklin. He lilted out the swinging chorus of the old buccaneer song in a rough but virile barytone that exactly suited the words and air, until the stockade walls echoed it back again.

As he swung down to the last low note there came a roar from the big shack ahead, the door was flung wide, and out into the yellow-lit space stumbled a giant figure that seemed to blink around in questioning.

"Darn your imperious nose!" growled Macklin. "Now you've done it. Come along and see if McShayne can quiet him."

A moment later they stood within the area of light from the open door. Before them was a big man with flaring black beard and unkempt hair, opening and closing his huge fists as he swayed unsteadily. He glared at them, unmindful of the bitter cold, and a growl of words issued from the tangle of beard.

"An' who may you be, spoilin' my luck? D'ye know who King Mont—"

Another figure darkened the doorway and broke in with a keen, curt voice of authority.

"Montenay, come inside, you fool! Do you want to freeze?

What cheer, Macklin! I've been looking for you. Hurry up, Montenay!"

Without a word of protest the giant turned and lurched inside. Radison guessed that he stood about six feet five, while his long, gorillalike arms swung almost to his knees.

As Barr Radison and Macklin stepped inside, the man at the door slammed it shut, and they threw off their heavy furs. The Canadian, used to similar scenes all his life, kept an attentive eye on the mumbling giant; but the tall American was frankly interested in the people surrounding him.

This was the last day of a wedding. In the big shack donated by the factor for the purpose were crowded the families of the Cree couple, who had evidently come in from their winter grounds with this express object. Two days earlier the missionary had done his work, which was the least part of the wedding in Cree eyes.

After the feast had come the dance, kept up with ever fresh vigor by fiddle and ancient concertina with every variety of known tune, from the Saskatchewan Circle to the Reel of Eight and back again. The few whites who took part out of politeness had long since given up the struggle, but the Crees were tireless. Order was preserved by McShayne, an ex-corporal of the Mounted, now in the company's service. In the corner beside him stood Montenay, glowering and growling.

Now there came a pause in the festivities, every one watching the newcomers, for Radison had got in only the night before, and had seen few about the post save the factor and McShayne.

In that first moment the tall American with the wide shoulders and prominent nose caused a whisper of "Moosewa!" and a laugh that rippled through the chunky squaws, but he did not hear this.

For him the squalid shack held only high romance, the lure of a strange land and a strange people, and as his keen, brown eyes met those of the Crees he smiled in sheer joy.

But there was etiquette to be observed, and Radison had

small chance to stare around him. McShayne seized his arm and turned him toward the bearded giant, for where dark men are there white men come always first.

"Shake hands with Barr Radison, Macferris Montenay. Radison's from the States, and came in last night with Macklin, here."

The cool, incisive tones of McShayne seemed to strike the giant into an amazed civility. He stuck out one hairy paw, then Radison felt the black eyes fixed on him in a peculiar glare, whether of liking or hate it was hard to determine.

"Radisson?" growled Montenay with a nasal twang. "Radisson? Sure, I'm not as far gone as that! Was it Radisson you said?"

"No," laughed Barr. "Radison—pure American, Montenay, and not French."

A puzzled look swept into the giant's face, and now Radison saw that he wore a belt that seemed made of bead-work, yet he had never seen such beads before. They were of a pure, lustrous white, interspersed with odd figures in red, lacked the usual backing of buckskin, and the whole affair was peculiar to Radison's eyes.

"But, man, ye spoiled my luck!" Montenay was looking down at him, an evil flame dancing in the bloodshot eyes. Macklin broke in at this instant, however, Montenay seemed to forget his thought, and Radison dismissed the whole matter as a drunken vagary. McShayne introduced him to the company in general, and to the bride's father in particular, and instantly all thought of Montenay dropped out of Radison's mind.

Uchichak, or the Crane, was a man of strength. From the narrow, almost Mongolian eyes to the vigorous mouth and firm chin, every line of his face bespoke crafty virility and power. His blanket capote was thrown open, but Radison saw that it was richly decorated in bead and quill work. The wiry black hair fell in a tufted strand on either side of his brown, sinewy neck.

As the American shook hands and met the steady, keen gaze

of the searching eyes he felt that Uchichak was one of the real Indians of days gone by, and to his surprise the chief spoke in almost flawless English.

"Welcome, man with strong eyes! You have brought gifts?"

To Radison's relief Macklin pushed forward and held out packages of tea and tobacco. The Crane accepted them with stolid dignity, as befitted the tribute to his superior qualities from these white men.

"Nothing slow about him," thought Radison with a chuckle. "He's as different from most of these low-browed Crees as day is from night."

Uchichak waved his hand at the waiting fiddler. Instantly the crowd broke into the "Drops of Brandy" with the enthusiasm of pent-up energy, while Radison and Macklin sought shelter in a corner. To his surprise, the American noted that Montenay was treated in a coldly polite manner by the Crees, as if he were a guest to be tolerated, but not to be encouraged or warmed up to.

"What did Montenay mean about his luck?" he asked the other. "And what's that belt he wears? Looks funny to me."

Take-a-chance grinned. "I guess he's the problem we're up against, Barr. At least, so the factor thinks. He'll be in hot water with these Crees if he doesn't watch out. Shut up and lay low for a while."

Radison nodded, though he did not understand. He knew that for two months and more he and Macklin had been tracing silver fox and black fox pelts, and had finally brought the quest to Fort Tenacity.

When there are "white tobacco" posts scattered about in open competition with the great company, no one is very much concerned, for the Indians know only one Ookimow, or great master.

But when the free-traders begin to send down skins of black and silver fox with monotonous regularity, at the rate of two or three every six months, and when the company's factor gets none in a year, then the company may be pardoned for desiring an explanation—and desiring it badly.

Such was the mission on which the two men had come; Macklin, because it lay in the line of duty, and Radison, because he had chanced upon the task and scented adventure. They had spent two months on the winter trail, going from post to post, from Indian village to lost hunters' shacks in the wilderness, vainly. Always had come the same answer from stalwart Ojibway and cunning-eyed Cree.

"*Kusketawukases? Sooneyowukases?* Neither black nor silver skins have we seen, my brothers, for many winters. Of a surety, we would take them to the great master, for is not the company our father?"

Finally they had gained a clue from a drunken Chipewa down at Lake Doobaunt, and the clue had led them to Tenacity, on the edge of the Empty Places, where there was daylight the whole summer through—half-light that knew no change, save when the lights turned all things grotesque.

That first month had been torture for the American. Unused to the country, the life, or the food, Radison had been racked from head to foot. At night he had sunk down helpless, and at morning he had donned his outer moccasins with a groan; but that was all past now. Toughened by the long trail from Fort Resolution, he had experienced the inevitable reaction of clean, hard living, rugged fare, and more rugged work.

Well was it for him that this was so, for now the clue promised to lead even beyond Fort Tenacity—on into the empty places where the snow was red; where Cree and Chipewa had swept out the Esquimaux. Not far from Tenacity was an independent post where Murphy, a free-trader, played a lone hand against long odds.

The Empty Places were being filled. First the Crees had pushed up, with a party of wandering Saulteaux. Then had come more Crees, and the Saulteaux had disappeared, for Ojibway blood is full of the wanderlust.

Afterward had come the Chipewa rovers, bringing with them certain women of the Saulteaux, so that the fate of the latter was in no doubt. This had started the trouble, although there is age-old feud in the souls of Chipewa and Cree, ready to flame out instantly; and after Tenacity was built, the wanderers, outcast from their people to the south, had pushed on once more to north and east, and in their trail the snow was red. So said the gossip of the northland, and Radison had come to look forward to these Empty Places with keen anticipation.

He and Macklin had reached the fort the night before, half their dogs dead, and with them a half-crazed runner bearing the mail, whom they had found perishing of hunger.

Radison had slept late in luxurious repose, then had fallen to work writing letters to go out before their trail had been covered. His sole family tie was the brother back in Baltimore, and Radison had no mind to sever all connections with the past. So he had yet seen little of the post itself, and Montenay had been a complete surprise to him.

He watched the big, heavily bearded giant as the dance proceeded. More than one Cree flashed a glance of quiet hatred at this white man who forced the women to dance with him, but Montenay paid little heed to such things.

Watching him, Radison was moved to give grudging admiration to the splendid physique of the man; and there was something fascinating about the high brow, strong bearded jaws, and massive features, though the eyes gleamed with a drunken leer.

Montenay seemed upheld by a tremendous pride, an arrogant sense of authority, which the American could not understand.

Suddenly Uchichak rose from his seat and lifted a hand. Upon the instant the fiddle ceased and the dancers fell away. As quiet settled down over the shack only the harsh breathing of Montenay could be heard, and the Crane flashed a look of contempt at him. The American leaned forward, keenly interested.

"There are many trails awaiting us, my brothers. Our lodges are far. Our traps call us, lest we fail in our debt to the Great Master and our lodges be empty of food. White Berries!"

The bride came forward and knelt at his feet, about her head the shawl which had been given her by Factor Campbell. Uchichak waited to be sure that every eye was fixed on him, then leaned down and kissed her.

"For the last time. Kiss now your husband, and after that no other man."

The groom, a stalwart young Cree, stepped forward, but another was ahead of him. Montenay, his eyes aflame, brushed him back with a drunken laugh.

"One first, Uchichak! Macferris Montenay owns this country, so, m'dear—"

A hoarse growl of rage quivered up from every throat; but even before the knife of the Crane whipped from its sheath, Montenay crashed down in his tracks. Over him stood Barr Radison, quivering with rage, and from his knuckles gathered a bright red drop that fell unheeded to the floor.

CHAPTER II

A CLUE OF MANY THREADS

WHILE THE serious-minded Macklin leaned over the map with Factor Campbell, Barr stretched back in his chair and stared at the log ceiling.

The stove was red-hot in the backroom of the trading store, and looking through to the larger room, Radison could see McShayne surrounded by squaws, who filled the space inside the long U-shaped counter.

Behind, on racks, and hung from the rafters, was every conceivable object, from sowbelly and blankets to painkiller and flintlock muskets.

Thinking over the events of the night before the American had almost concluded that a certain Macferris Montenay was not right in his head. It was peculiar, mused Radison, that after he had knocked Montenay down the giant had made no offensive move.

He had raised himself on one elbow, stared up at his assailant, whom he could have broken across one knee, with a queer, almost frightened expression and a mutter about his "luck." Suddenly Barr realized that Macklin was speaking to him.

"Here, old man, the evidence is all in, and you'd better get the result of the inquest. Give him what you know about the pelts, factor."

"I know nothing about 'em," Campbell grunted. "It's all news to me, and if such furs are going out, then Murphy must get them from the Chipewas. None of the Crees go near the Ookimasis, or Small Master, as they call him, and he caters to the Chipewas; we get a good deal of the Chipewa trade, just the same."

"Where does Montenay get his liquor?" shot out Take-a-chance. "Murphy?"

"No, nor from me," returned Campbell sturdily. "Whatever he does, Murphy is clean in that respect. As for Montenay, he's been up here for years. Where he came from no one knows; but he's a big man among the Chipewas, though I doubt if he's a squaw-man.

"Once in a while he blows in here with some common pelts, seems to have plenty of liquor, and is eternally chanting that fool song of his—calls it his 'luck.' The Crees hate him like poison, but I never could learn just why. They don't talk much about what happens out yonder, you know.

"The missionary expects to get a church up this summer; but, Lord, the Crees don't bother with religion since old Père Sulvent vanished! He was the boy could hand it to 'em!"

"Who's he?" queried Radison. "What do you mean by vanished?"

"Same as the dictionary," came the curt answer. "Sulvent was a Frenchman, with Irish blood. He went out on a trip six months ago, when the darkness had come; but he never came back. He'd handed it to Montenay pretty heavy just before, and that may have something to do with the Crees' hatred; but I don't know. Maybe it was frost got him; maybe a bullet."

Macklin nodded, frowning, and Radison's eyes glistened.

"Do you mean there's actual war out there?"

"The Lord only knows what's out there, Radison, and that's the truth," returned the factor wearily. "The Empty Places are hell; I've been out once or twice; but it's too much for me. Montenay always strikes off to the northeast, and a man must have the fear of God or the devil in him to make that trip alone. Murphy lives there, on the edge of things, and he often comes over here with his daughter—"

"Daughter?" broke in Macklin. "Does the fool take a chance like that? Is she a breed?"

The factor shook his head sourly. "No—our kind. She's lived there for a year, now; Père Sulvent got him to send her back to Quebec to school. That was years ago, before my time here; but I've heard that she was born up here, and her mother died, after Murphy started his God-forsaken post.

"It's my idea that Montenay lords it over the Chipewas, for when he's drunk he calls himself 'King Montenay,' and Murphy seems to know him pretty well."

"What's that belt of his, Campbell?" asked the American. Macklin grinned.

"That's what we all want to know, Barr! The factor swears that it's wampum—the original shell wampum like the old Injuns used to make down south. That's all rot, though."

"Don't be too sure, Take-a-chance," retorted Campbell. "Four months ago, with the first snow, a Chipewa came in to get credit with us. He carried a rifle, but besides that he had a flintlock pistol. Where did he get it?"

"Murphy, of course," said Macklin. The factor grunted disgustedly.

"Murphy don't trade pistols stamped with the *Fleur-de-lis* and the date 1704," was his dry answer. The others stared at him.

"Do you mean to say that a two-hundred-year-old flintlock pistol can still be in use?" demanded the Canadian.

"Aye, perfect in every way. The Chipewa refused to trade it, and said he carried it as big medicine.

"Now, there's something almighty queer out there, boys, and Macferris Montenay is behind it. He's no fool, that man. Any one who can win the hatred and respect of these Crees about here, and still live to enjoy it, is going some.

"Where that wampum belt or that pistol came from, I don't know; the old French and English traders were never up here, to my knowledge. But if all them black and silver pelts go out every year, I'd either say that somebody is a blamed liar or else Montenay has a fox farm—which don't fit exactly."

"No," laughed Radison, "a fox farm doesn't fit in with Montenay very well. I'm inclined to think the man is crazy, myself."

"The Crees call him Crazy Bear to his face," chuckled Campbell. "That suits him, all right. Well, that covers all I know. I've sent for Uchichak—hello! Here's the chief now, to a dot!"

"What cheer!"

In the doorway appeared the Crane, his woolen capote slashed with red on arms and hips, a gay scarlet sash about his waist. He gravely shook hands with the three, then pulled out his pipe and sat down. Without preamble Macklin divulged his story for the benefit of the Cree, whom Campbell declared they could trust thoroughly.

Uchichak listened in silence. Several times Radison caught the beady eyes fixed on him, and remembered the wordless handclasp he had received after the affair of the previous night. The Crane was a man who spoke little, and when Macklin stated that Radison was with him there came a little gesture of inquiry.

"He is my friend," replied Macklin. "He is an American, from the States; not of the company, but to be trusted. He is a man, my brother."

The chief bowed his head gravely and Macklin went on. Suddenly the dark face flashed up and the deep, even voice broke in.

"Wait. Has my brother seen these pelts of which he speaks? Are they fresh, or are they old?"

"By thunder!" ejaculated the other quickly, "I clear forgot about that, factor! I saw one of them down at Winnipeg. It was hard, very dry, and creased pretty deep, as if it had been laid away for a long while. No, it wasn't fresh at all, Uchichak, but it was in prime condition just the same."

The chief puzzled over this inscrutably until his pipe and the story were concluded together. Campbell handed him a plug of tobacco, which he stowed away after whittling off another pipeful.

"It is well, my brothers. Do you wish to follow Crazy Bear when he departs?"

"That seems to be the only thing to do," returned Macklin doubtfully. "How about dogs? What's left of ours are all to the bad, and our sled is pretty well banged up."

"Uchichak has the best dogs around here," put in the factor. The dark eyes gleamed with pride and the Cree nodded.

"The Crane will go," he decided quietly. "But my young men must follow us. We must take with us food and powder for a long time. The journey will be a very bad one; but not even Crazy Bear will dare to harm one of the company, and the others will fear. We must follow in secret while my young men are gathering. That will take time, my brothers, for they are on their fur-grounds now."

"They shall not lose by it," promised Macklin. "Their debt for this year shall be wiped off the books. Yes, we must follow in secret, and then come to him openly as if we were surveying for the company. If we can persuade him to throw those pelts to us, and perhaps find out where they come from, there will be more rewards for you and your men, Uchichak."

"*Miwasin!* Good!" returned the chief, his eyes glittering. Campbell grunted, for such wholesale promises were not at all to his liking and promised to make wild confusion with his books. Still, orders were orders, and Macklin was to have a free hand in everything that he wished.

Radison knew that the Crane would be a powerful aid to them in their quest. In thus deciding to strike off on the trail of Montenay into the Empty Places they were attempting a desperate venture, and from what they could learn of these same Empty Places they were likely to run into trouble.

Neither man was of the stamp to hesitate on that account, however, and it was unbelievable that Montenay would dare offer violence to any men directly in the company's service.

Such a thing was unheard of, even in these days when the north country is open to all traders alike; for, although the wastes have changed hands, it has not changed masters, and every "nichie" from Rupert to the Great Bear is fully aware of the fact.

Now, the Crane and Tom Macklin put their heads together, while Campbell made out the list they would require from his stores. The largest item, of course, was frozen whitefish for the dogs, the chief priding himself on his team and regarding them above all else, which was well, for three men's lives might depend on those dogs ere Montenay was run down to his lair.

The Indian's heart was made glad by the gift of the extra rifle which Macklin had brought. The company trade-guns are good weapons enough for hunting and fur-killing, but for such a trip as lay before them it was more fitting that the chief should carry a rifle. Also, as Campbell grunted, it was safer.

"Nonsense," laughed Radison easily, rising and stretching himself. "We're not leading any war-party, Campbell. There's no harm in paying Montenay a visit, and I don't mind saying that I'd like to have a look at that freetrader's post."

"Yes—her name is Noreen," chuckled the factor. "The Injuns call her Minebegonequay—Girl-with-flowers-in-her-hair."

"Get out of here, you old humbug!" added Macklin with a grin. "We have something else to think of if you haven't. Take a chance on meeting your friend Montenay, and get along with you!"

Radison laughed easily and strolled into the outer room, where McShayne had got rid of the squaws and was bartering with one of the Crane's men. To tell the truth, he had not had the free-trader's daughter in mind when he spoke, but he carried the name out with him reflectively.

Noreen—it was not hard to guess at Trader Murphy's mother country. As to the Indian title, Radison already knew enough about northern nomenclature to make a shrewd guess that Noreen Murphy was either red or golden-haired. Therefore, she must be pretty; and Murphy was a fool to keep her up here in the wastes.

Rather pleased with his own deductions, Barr filled his pipe from McShayne's plug and put a question or two to him about the Empty Places. The ex-trooper watched the Cree go out, flung the pelts behind the counter, and emitted a growl.

"Wanted nothing but powder! That crazy fool Montenay will get a bullet in the back yet. Why, as to the Empty Places, every one talks and no one knows anything. I've heard say that the Spirit Dancers live out there in the hills.

"You don't know what the Spirit Dancers are? Why, the northern lights—that's what the nichies call the lights. Think they're ghosts, I s'pose. Dunno's I blame them much. Take 'em sometimes and they sure do look humanlike, especially if a man's on a lonesome trail and kind o' off his head."

McShayne could or would say little about the red snow, however, except that out in the wastes anything might take place. Barr gathered that the post stood in what might be termed neutral ground, which accounted for Montenay's visits. The actual conflict, if conflict there were, would be more apt to happen out on the lonely hunting-grounds, and those at Tenacity knew nothing of it save when some hunter failed to take up his debt.

"That's the devil of it," concluded the aggrieved corporal. "It wouldn't matter how much they scrap if them as gets killed only left life-insurance, but they don't. Last winter as many as a dozen accounts had to be put down to loss. Good thing Murphy won't sell 'em liquor on the sly, like some freetraders do."

Where, then, did Macferris Montenay get his liquor? That question was flitting through Radison's mind as he nodded to McShayne and stepped to the door. Evidently the giant had some secret supply of his own.

As he emerged into the sunlight the American halted abruptly. A dozen feet away stood Montenay himself, calmly smoking a pipe as he worked over a broken snow-shoe. Barr tensed his muscles for instant action, but to his surprise the other merely nodded amiably.

"'Mornin'!" Montenay set down the long shoe, leaning carelessly on it as he met the eyes of Radison. "Name's Radisson—or do I misremember?"

At this astonishing greeting Radison chuckled to himself.

"Speak it English fashion, Montenay. It's not Radisson, but Radison, and I'm no Frenchman. I thought you might be wanting to punch my head this morning."

To the half-quizzical look that accompanied these words Montenay replied with a slow shake of the head, his face serious.

"Young man, that blow o' last night saved Macferris Montenay from a Cree knife, belike, an' I bear ye no ill-will—for that. From the States, eh? I was part ways under liquor, but I remember that plain enough. Also, ye spoiled my luck, an' I remember that."

A puzzled look flashed into Radison's face as he gazed at the big fellow and met the dark, passionate eyes.

"If you call that old pirate song your 'luck,' you're off your base. Why on earth don't you learn the right tune if you want to sing it? As to the other matter, I'm glad that you aren't out after my blood, for, to tell the truth, I'd rather let you scrap with some one else."

Montenay did not respond to the laughing words for a moment. No light answered from his heavy face, and he stared at the other with that same serious, somber air.

"Ever chance to hear o' him that founded the Hungry Belly Company?"

"Who?" asked the puzzled American.

"Why, him that found the Mississip', him that vanished somewheres—him, the friend o' kings an' king o' Hudson Bay while he lasted, before they betrayed him?"

"You don't mean the Canadian, Pierre Radisson?"

"Aye, but I do! Pierre the Great he was. Listen, now! Go back where ye came from, Radisson; don't think the prophecy is so easy carried out, even if ye do bear his name."

With which enigmatic speech the big man flung the snow-shoe over his shoulder and tramped away, leaving Radison standing in blank wonder.

Montenay was crazy, certainly. That was the only solution, and for an instant Barr felt troubled over their journey after him. That he himself bore the name of Pierre Radisson might be true, though he had no thought that he was a descendant of the old explorer.

One or two squaws of the Crane's party, flitting silently by, threw admiring glances at him, and with an answering wave of his hand Radison dismissed the vexing problem of Macferris Montenay.

"I'm glad to be alive!" he muttered, looking upward at the sky. "Glad to be here! Glad to be in this new world! I think—I think that I have come to be proven at last in the midst of snow and crazy men!"

With a little sigh of humorous contentment he relit his pipe and turned back into the store. He did not notice that the squaws had suddenly veered from the shadow of a small, lithe man in the stockade gateway, a man who wore moccasins of Chipewa cut, and who defiantly filled his pipe from a whittled plug of "white" tobacco in the very gateway of the "black" tobacco post.

CHAPTER III

ON THE TRAIL

SPAT! *Spat!*
Still dreaming of Broadway, Radison awoke. He laughed aloud as the log rafters overhead recalled him to the Northland, and his laughter was echoed by another dull whip-crack, loud in the frost without.

"Must have fallen asleep while I waited," he muttered, sitting up with a yawn. "Hello! This looks something like!"

He went to the window, and stood there in awe as the purple light blazed dimly on his face. Many times had he seen the lights, but never like this.

Across the sky flitted grotesque-sheeted figures of lambent flame, dancing, whirling, flinging many-colored ribbons in what appeared wild confusion—yet to the American it seemed that there was something methodical, something human behind it all.

Up and across and back again the fires flashed, as if some unseen hand were playing on a mighty keyboard in a vast harmony of colorings.

"Radison! Get your shoes—here's the chief!"

Barr came back to earth with a start as the voice of Macklin rang out, followed by a yapping of dogs. Turning, he slipped into his thick blanket capote, knotted the sash, and drew up the hood. Then he took his moosehide-cased rifle, emerged from the shack, and got into his snow-shoes, upturned at the toes in Ojibway fashion. Take-a-chance Macklin and Uchichak were standing beside a heavily laden dog-sled, waiting.

Six hours before Montenay had departed with his team alone, as he had come. What preparations the Crane had made Radison did not know, for the chief had vanished after that talk in the store the morning previous.

That Montenay suspected the errand of Macklin and Barr did not appear. In fact, none knew of it save the factor and Uchichak, and Montenay had asked no questions. He had brought in pelts to the value of thirty skins—a "skin" being a dollar in the north—and had taken in exchange, to the utter mystification of Campbell and McShayne, a load of such delicacies as tinned goods, beef extract, and unadulterated tea.

"The devil must be settin' up housekeeping," had growled the ex-trooper. "Why didn't he go to Murphy for 'em? I wonder. He's never got such stuff here before."

"He may have his eye on Minebegonequay," suggested Campbell in heavy facetiousness and with a sly glance at Radison. "Better make a trip over there, Rad. You might spoil his luck in another direction."

"Not on your life!" laughed Barr. "I'm no trouble-hunter!"

Now, in impressive gravity, the factor and his assistant came out to see the party off. There was a handshake all around, Macklin nodded, the chief cracked his whip and emitted an equally snappy *mash*, and the dogs leaned forward on the traces.

Handing over the whip to Macklin, Uchichak preceded the team more from custom than from necessity. Radison saw at once that they were following a newly broken trail. He did not need the finger of Macklin pointing at the oval-shaped snow-shoe track to know whose it was.

"There have been no sundogs," declared the Canadian confidently. "We'll probably have a clear run all the way, so it's safe to give him his six-hour start and take our time. We don't want to catch him till after he's reached home, wherever that is."

The daylike night was coming on bitterly cold, and it was not long before all three covered their faces up to the eyes. Uchichak did not hurry, for the sled was heavy with fish and pemmican bricks and other things—such as cartridges.

That their run would be a long one all knew well; but the march was a silent and ceaseless "sluff-sluff" over the snow, until Radison exclaimed in wonder at a particularly brilliant flare of the lights, which shot red and green far above the zenith.

"They are the Spirit Dancers," affirmed the Cree solemnly. "Crazy Bear prays to them, and his Chipewa braves make big medicine. We know that they are only the spirits of the dead watching over their children, the Naeyowuk (Crees)."

With a slight gesture of contempt the stalwart chief swung ahead, his bronze face immobile. Macklin turned with a grin and a low mutter of words.

"Montenay prays to 'em, eh? Looks like we're up against something ugly, Barr. Wouldn't be surprised if he had started some newfangled religion up here among the Chipewas. We may have a second Riel rebellion on our hands, north of the circle!"

Radison did not reply. So Montenay prayed to the Spirit Dancers—why? Was the man really crazed? What was the meaning of his allusion to the "prophecy"? But there was no answer to his questionings, and the three slapped along in silence while the slow miles slipped behind them.

They had left the Arkilinik behind, and with the passing of the river only jack-pine and spruce and snow-barrens stretched around in wild wastes that had no end and no beginning.

"Is the free-trader's post anywhere near here?" asked Radison suddenly. Macklin shook his head, but the chief answered from in front.

"It is a day and a half from the black tobacco house. Crazy

Bear travels fast toward it. To-morrow we will meet Niska, one of my young men, at the Wusap. There we will rest and gain news."

Wusap Lake, according to the map Radison had seen in the factor's store, lay northeast of the post some fifty miles. Beyond this lay the "white tobacco house"—so called because the free-traders sell the light-colored plug, that of the company being dark in color.

Ever as they trudged onward, the Spirit Dancers leaped and twisted across the sky, and a faint rumbling as of distant thunder came out of the dim north. Hour after hour fled past, and still the "sluff-sluff" of the shoes went on at an even, tireless pace. The team of huskies was a magnificent one, and Radison knew they could overhaul the bearded giant if Uchichak was so minded.

It was not until after midnight that they halted in a little clump of twisted jack-pine. There was no deep snow among the trees, and they soon had made camp. Radison had already noted that the Cree wore Ojibway shoes like his own, and now Uchichak built a conical fire, standing the sticks on end.

"Some Chipewa might be hanging around," explained Macklin, throwing a fish each to the dogs. "If he saw a Cree trail or a Cree fire on Montenay's trail he'd get suspicious; but if he finds our tracks or this fire he'd lay it to a Saulteaux party. The Saulteaux wander all over, and get up here now and then. They're willing to take a chance on being wiped out—and they take considerable chance up in this country."

The halt was short—only a smoke, to give the dogs a rest and to make a cup of tea. Then they sped on again, hour after hour, and gradually the Spirit Dancers faded out into faint silver streamers that slowly died away into nothing.

The American was striding along behind the sled, followed by Macklin, when he saw Uchichak suddenly fling up his hood, throwing back his head to listen for an instant. Radison glanced about quickly, but the waste of snow and scattered tree-clumps was as lonely as ever, and if the Indian's keen senses had caught some warning flicker of shadow or branch, it did not come to the others.

From near and far the frost was cracking the trees, for there had been a slight thaw the day before, and the limbs were sending forth reports that rang like pistol-shots.

That Uchichak had caught a warning became evident five minutes later. One of the dogs uttered a quick, short howl, commenced floundering in the snow, and within a moment the entire team was in a snarling tangle of bodies. Leaving the others to attend to the dogs, Uchichak caught up his cased rifle from the sled and whirled about.

Radison thought that he caught a faint gun-shot drifting to them, but it might have been frost in the trees. The snowy wastes were bare as ever and there was nothing in sight to indicate any enemy; but when Radison turned to Macklin the other had straightened out the team, and one dog lay dead, shot through the body and freezing already.

"This looks like business, chief," exclaimed Take-a-chance quietly. He sent a thin-lipped, mirthless grin at the American. "I guess that's a pretty plain hint to mind our own business, eh?"

"Who from—Montenay?"

"Lord knows! But I doubt it. Sounded like a trade-musket; pretty distant shot, and it was evidently meant for the Crane. Hello! Going to camp?"

Uchichak was already squatting over some twigs and a shred of birch-bark. He answered without looking up, in a voice that sounded like the snarl of a dog.

"Stop one smoke. Rest the dogs."

No sooner had he swallowed a cup of scalding hot tea than the Crane took up his rifle and slipped away over the snows toward the left. Radison filled his pipe and settled down beside his comrade, who seemed to take the happening with calm unconcern.

"You're an emotionless sort of beast, Mack! Think he'll find any one?"

"No." Macklin shrugged his shoulders. "Wants to find which way the beggar went. I'd take a chance that it wasn't Montenay, though. What's the matter—tired?"

"Not a bit. Just thinking, that's all."

He stared out over the snows, absently watching the distant figure of the Crane. His companion threw a quick glance at him, but ventured no comment. After a moment the American turned with a grunt and flung an entirely useless twig on the fire.

"Funny how some things will bring back other things, entirely different, isn't it?"

"Hope the chief brings back something that looks like a Chipewa," returned the Canadian curtly. Radison smiled.

"You know I don't mean that. Stop your fooling, Mack. I just thought of something that I'd forgotten all about for six years. I had left home at nineteen, and after a bit I got mighty sick of the tourists I was with in Spain.

"I skipped the bunch at Cordova and went up to Madrid with a mule-train—through a damned desolate part of Spain, too. Well, one morning a mule died. That was all.

"I hadn't thought about it for years, but somehow this brings the whole scene back to me—the little line of mules, me with my camera, Pedro and Vasquez cursing like devils as they changed the packs about, and a solitary *guardia civile* riding past across that sun-damned plain."

He paused, staring morosely into the fire. Macklin was frankly puzzled by his mood, for there was nothing of the dreamer in his rugged nature. After a moment he removed the pipe from his mouth and waved it at the dogs.

"What's the sunny land of Spain got to do with this? And why the blue streak? I don't quite get the connection, Barr."

"Because it brought me back to where I was then—made me realize the years between, that's all. There's no connection, of course; only this scene happened to bring back the other one. Makes me think of the six years' difference in myself."

"Huh! You ain't exactly cheerful over it. Been murdering anybody? Stole anything? Broke any hearts?" The bantering tone suddenly became earnest. "Got a girl anywheres?"

"No," laughed Radison. "It's only that I'm getting old, Mack. Lord, no! Not remorse, or anything like that—simply that I'll never be nineteen again. I've lost my grip on youth, and I wish that I had those six years back."

Suddenly comprehending, the other knocked his pipe out against his moccasin.

"Listen, Barr. You ain't lost much in that six years, I guess. You've been decent, I mean; you've been doing things; you've been growing all the while?"

"On the outside, yes. But I'm not so sure about the inside. I don't look at things now the way I did then—well, it's hard to explain."

"Shucks! You need some sass'fras tea. Why, you can't grow on the outside unless you grow inside first. Ain't that right? As for looking at things, wait till you're fifty or so; if you look at 'em half-way decent by that time, you'll be in pretty safe shape to take the last trail. Why, you ain't full-grown up yet, partner! Talking about losing your grip on youth—rats! All you need to do is to reach out and grab her again—like getting your second wind."

"Maybe you're right," and Barr hesitated a moment, biting his lips. "But I'm a useless sort of cuss to everybody except myself. Six years—and it's gone unnoticed!"

"Well, you wouldn't expect it to rise up and whack you over the head, would you? But here's the chief coming back, so we'll adjourn the meeting for a bit."

Radison, flinging off his mood, emptied his pipe and rose to meet the tall figure of Uchichak. The latter had circled around behind and came in from the right; now, in response to their questioning looks, he shook his head.

"There is a *usam* trail, but there is no time to follow now."

"Chipewa snowshoe?" asked Barr. The chief nodded grimly.

"To our right, leading east. If I had struck to right instead of left, my brothers, I might have gained a shot. Kisamunito, the Master of Life, has spared him to another day. It is well."

Uchichak philosophically strapped his rifle on the sled and caught up the dog-whip, Macklin now breaking trail. A light, keen wind was sweeping down across the barrens, but Macklin pushed up the pace and they were soon all aglow.

Silently, putting all their heart into the work, they pushed on through the morning, and at noon came to a narrow stretch of ice, bordered with heavy, snow-burdened pine and spruce. This Uchichak stated to be an arm of Wusap Lake, and here they halted.

After the kettle boiled and the frozen pemmican was soft, the Crane flung a handful of old birch-bark on the fire. Up darted one full puff of smoke, and the next instant he scattered the small blaze with his foot.

"The Goose is near by," he deigned to explain, "and Niska is cunning of eye."

Radison settled down to wait, and the three held a low discussion as to the slayer of the dog that morning. It was finally decided that it must have been a Chipewa who had wandered on their track, and that after the shot he had fled on ahead toward his own people.

Without the slightest warning, the bushes on the opposite side of the ice, fifty feet away, opened and an Indian stepped confidently toward them. Guessing from the calm demeanor of the chief that the newcomer was Niska, or the Goose, Radison watched the short, sinewy man approach.

"What cheer!" was his greeting, to which the three answered as one. Then came a rapid dialogue between the two Crees. Niska's face darkened, and he gave an angry exclamation, but Uchichak turned to his companions.

"The Goose passed a breed from the south—a man named

Nichemus, who dwells with the Chipewas," he said. "It was he who killed the dog. Also, the man must have followed us from the post. Five miles ahead is a camp of ten Chipewas. Crazy Bear is with them."

Macklin uttered a grunt at this surprising information.

"He had us spotted, Barr. We'd better join him openly, chief,"

"No." Uchichak shook his head. "The Goose overheard their talk, and it was not of us. They have some other plan on foot, my brothers. Crazy Bear looks toward the white tobacco-house for a squaw."

"I feel sorry for Murphy's girl, then," stated Radison, and he felt oddly disappointed. Minebegonequay was a pretty name.

Finally it was decided that Niska should return, gather what Crees he could, and meet them at Murphy's. In case Montenay made any trouble, which Macklin did not expect, a few braves might came in handy; besides, as the Crane said, the absence of the Chipewas from their fur-grounds looked suspicious.

"The chief and I will take a scout ahead, and maybe drop in on Crazy Bear," concluded Macklin. "You stay here and rest up, old man. This affair don't look just right."

Niska finished off the tea and pemmican and started on the back trail. Barr made no objection to Macklin's proposal, for the hard trail had worn him out and he was glad to rest. Besides, the Canadian knew his own business best.

Five minutes later Uchichak and Macklin departed, sweeping out to the left in a wide circle. Radison built up his fire again, rolled up in his blanket, and was fast asleep in a moment, too weary even to smoke.

CHAPTER IV

JEAN NICHEMUS

"**I** T'INK ME he's be one ver' fine gun—make for keel one, two mile off, mebbe." The liquid, reflective words were followed by a swift, vicious kick in the side that jarred Radison awake instantly. Flinging his blanket wide, he sat up and stared in puzzled wonder at the speaker.

Brown of face, yet far lighter than an Indian, the man was small, wide-shouldered, and plainly possessed tremendous strength beneath his dirty white capote. The hood of the latter extended over his head in two points, like lynx ears, and on the front were worked rude eyes in red beads and quill which lent him a striking appearance, to say the least.

It was not this that caused Radison's wonder, however, for the man was coolly regarding him over the sights of his own rifle, whose casing lay on the snow at his side. The American frowned, comprehending.

"What's this—a hold-up? Who the devil are you?"

"Be ver' quiet!" The warning voice held a menace that could not be mistaken, and Barr sat still. A glance around showed that his fire had not died down, so that his companions had not been long away.

He remembered the message of Niska—this man must be the breed, Nichemus! No doubt he had followed the Goose back, had seen the departure of Macklin and Uchichak, and had descended upon the camp forthwith. Yet surely there must be some mistake, thought the American; this hunter would never dare attack men in the service of the company.

"Are you Nichemus?" he asked.

"*Oui*, Jean Nichemus, *m'sieu!*" The breed grinned. "*B'jou, b'jou!*"

"Put down that gun," commanded Barr quietly. "Do you know that I am in the employ of the company? What do you mean by this?"

Nichemus quickly slid back a few paces, but held the rifle steady.

"By Goss, you be quiet!" Again the glittering eye warned Radison. "We don' got no p'leece by dis place! W'at I mean, hey? You fin' dat out ver' soon, Meestair Radisson. You go for make scrap, de Crane, he fin' one dead man on de cam'."

The humor of the situation struck Radison oddly, and he laughed.

"All right, Jean; I won't start anything, since you have the drop on me. Now suppose you get down to cases. What're you holding me up this way for? Don't you know that if the company turns on you it can drive you into the ground like a rat?"

"De comp'ny— Here before Chris', hey?" There was a note of supreme contempt in the voice of Nichemus as he used the slang phrase for the H. B. C., which held more truth than most slang phrases. "W'at do I care for de comp'ny? She's be de one beeg cheat, dat comp'ny."

"Well, what in thunder do you want of me?" cried the exasperated American.

"You," came the cool retort. "De king he's say to me, 'Go for catch dat Radisson. Don' keel, jus' catch.' So I come on de cam'; now we go see de king."

Radison stared at him, bewildered.

"Say," he gasped at length, "is every one crazy up here, or am I off my head? What king are you talking about, Nichemus? You'd better get a move on and clear out of here before Uchichak gets back."

The breed's face darkened.

"I t'ink me you be de one beeg fool. Mebbe you nevair hear of Mont'nay? Now you get up, or I shoot."

In a flash Radison understood.

Montenay! The giant had sent this breed to get him without injury, for some purpose that could not be guessed, but Radison had no mind to obey such a peremptory summons. He glanced about the camp with a smile.

"Shoot your blamed head off, Jean," he returned cheerfully. "You won't budge me out of here; so you can forget that part of it."

"So?" The other nodded toward a twig snapped out from the fire, lying within an inch of Radison's hand. Before the American guessed his purpose the rifle shifted and spat flame; as the sharp crack echoed over the barrens and brought him up, startled, he saw that the twig had vanished. Instantly Nichemus jerked out the shell and covered him again grimly.

"You see? Mebbe you come now, hey? Nex' time I make for hit your han'—one finger go lak de twig."

There was no mistaking the earnestness of his voice, the uncompromising, deadly eyes that looked over the rifle-sights. Radison merely nodded and got to his feet, for Jean Nichemus was plainly not a man to be trifled with and fear of the great company lay not in his heart.

Radison began to realize that if Montenay was a maniac, he was unusually sane for a crazy man; also, that Jean Nichemus was like to prove worthy of his master.

"Well, Jean, what next?" he said with a grimace as he rose.

The breed lowered his rifle, regarding the American curiously. In turn, Barr took in the sensitive yet brutal face, the dark, liquid eyes, heavy lidded with strength and cunning, and the coarse black hair that was almost the only trace of the man's motherhood—that and the eyes.

It occurred to Radison that the rifleshot might serve to recall his comrades, but the breed must have known they were safe from interruption or he would not have fired. With a little gesture of decision Nichemus stooped for the rifle-case.

"*M'sieu,* you give me your parole—ver good, den we go for see de king."

"And if I don't?"

"*Non?* Den we go, anyhow."

Radison's jaw set aggressively for a moment; he was not used to receiving orders in this fashion, and it rasped him the wrong way instantly. Then the cool, determined manner of the breed was borne in on him, and he assented.

"Very well. I give you my parole until we reach Montenay— and if you think he's a king you're very much mistaken. Wait till Macklin comes back and you'll see your king jump down off his perch mighty quick, Jean!"

The other only grinned cheerfully, cased the rifle, picked up his own musket, and untied his snow-shoes, which he handed to Radison.

"Put dem on, *m'sieu,* an' follow my trail back. I t'ink me dat Uchichak be one ver''stonishe' fellair, *non?*"

Radison was not so sure that Uchichak would be puzzled, but the ruse would, at least, serve to hold Macklin and the Crane here for a time on their return. Radison swung off on the trail of the breed, while Jean slipped on the American's shoes and followed, carefully covering the trail, in order to make the others think that Barr had gone out alone.

That he was in any danger from Montenay never entered the head of Radison, and yet he was decidedly worried over this abrupt and forceful summons. The more he had seen of Montenay, the more he liked other company, and the fact that Nichemus seemed to have an all-abiding trust in his master's power was by no means reassuring.

Barr Radison had seen a good deal of other men with the mask off. He had gone through the Cotabatos with a dozen lost troopers, he had found Sokotra with a motorboat and well nigh stayed there, he had braved the Lorian Swamp with two daredevil Afrikanders, and he knew that Jean Nichemus was just plain *man,* every inch of him, and not quite up to his own mark when it came to that. But Montenay was different. Drunk, Montenay was a gorilla. Sober—

"God knows!" he thought to himself, "when Montenay is sober he's either stark mad, which isn't to be wondered at in this country, or he's a good deal more of a man than I've ever met before. I think we'll have quite an interesting bit of conversation, Mr. Macferris Montenay—and if you try to come any of that king business on me, there'll be more than conversation!"

With a little scorn of the man, he looked back to see Nichemus crunching down over the tracks he left, sweeping them as he strode with the tasseled end of his rifle-case and obliterating every trace of the shoes worn by the American. Though the cunning swiftness of the work was admirable, Radison knew that neither Macklin nor Uchichak would be deceived into thinking that only one man had come and gone.

"It's second nature to him, that's all," he concluded as he followed the oval tracks that Nichemus had left in reaching the camp. "He's on dangerous business, and he covers the trail just as Macklin stamps a burned match into the snow, from force of habit; one's about as useless as the other, but at certain times it may mean everything."

Across the lake they went, while overhead the Spirit Dancers sent long, shuddering, grotesque shadows moving all around them; the woods seemed peopled with quivering life, and as they drove up the hill beyond and through the trees that stretched dark and silent ahead, a strange sense of oppression began to fall upon Radison.

Soon the woods were all about them, and that indefinable oppression leaped into something very like fear as from the distance, thin and clear and sharp, rose a single whine that deepened suddenly—"Whi-i-i-i-mbuh! Whi-i-i-i-m-buh-h-h!" Then another and another and another joined in, until all finished with one swift "Ghur-r-r—yap!" that struck eery echoes from the silent places and was no more.

"You damn fool!" muttered Barr, rubbing his mitten against his hood to wipe the sweat from his brow. "To let a wolf-howl get your goat like that! Buck up here and get ready to lam the spots out of that Montenay!"

With an effort he shook the chill from his heart and became

himself again, alert and self-contained as he swung forward on the trail, exchanging no word with Nichemus.

When he knew that they must have covered five miles, he was puzzled; Niska had said that Crazy Bear was five miles ahead, but they had seen no sign of life. A few moments later, however, they crossed another narrow tongue of ice, showing that they were still near the lake, and came to a deserted, fireless camping-place.

Radison took the broad trail that went on ahead, and Nichemus merely grunted his assent, so he concluded that Montenay was waiting for them farther on. The breed made no effort at concealment now, but came steadily along.

Suddenly he growled out a word of warning, swept around and took the lead. Five minutes later he flung up a hand, and upon reaching his side Radison halted, to stare in amazement at the scene before them.

They stood on the brow of a little declivity. A dozen feet below, and twice as many away, was a clump of figures with two dog-sleds. Montenay's huge fur hood rose high over the rest, and his deep voice reached Radison in a rumble of sound that had no meaning, for it was evidently the Chipewa tongue.

Though their arrival must have been heard, not a figure stirred save among the dogs, who uttered one or two yaps as they scented the stranger.

Suddenly Montenay flung up his arms and broke out into English, his rime-whitened tangle of beard thrown upward.

"O Spirits of the Dead, Watchers of the King, prosper me your servant this night! Even as the Silent Ones who sit yonder, you, their spirits, hear me! Let the prophecy be vain for this time, O Dead!"

A startled gasp broke from the group below. As if answering Montenay, one vivid arrow of crimson leaped up to the zenith and was gone, the green and purple fires playing as before in its place.

Suddenly Radison felt a nudge, saw that the Chipewas had

broken apart, and in utter bewilderment at what he had seen and heard he strode forward to meet Montenay, who had turned to greet him with outstretched hand.

"So, Radisson, ye had to come?"

The American gripped the other's hand, feeling that the spell of the thing had rendered him powerless to resist. But there was no animosity in the face of Montenay; rather, the great eyes were filled with a mingled eagerness and strange wistful longing, and his hand held that of Radison for a tense minute.

"I'd like to know what warrant you had for taking me prisoner," returned Barr quietly.

"Warrant? Why—but that can come later. I need you, Radisson—I wanted ye to be with me, to grip and grip, share and share with me. Man, but I like ye fine! Tell me, what brought you up here?"

"I don't think this is any place to discuss our business," rejoined Radison decisively. "You might send out for Macklin and—"

"None o' them go with me this night! Tell me, was it the Silent Ones called you here?"

"Silent Ones?" Radison repeated the words, puzzled. "If you must have it, we came up here to trace a number of silver fox—"

"Ho, ho!" Montenay threw back his head in a great laugh. "It was the pelts, eh? Lord bless me, but I'm a fool! That's what comes to a man when he gets fear into his bones, Radisson; I've been fearing that you'd come for a year past, but now you're here—I want ye for a friend."

Radison looked at him in silence. Mad as the words seemed, Montenay's voice and aspect were certainly sane enough. He decided that it would be folly to provoke the man, but he had no mind for meek acquiescence.

"I don't pretend to understand what you're driving at; but, as I have no reason to bear animosity against you, I don't see why there should be any between us. None the less, I can't go off and leave my party this way."

"They'll know what's happened, never fear," chuckled the other. "But before they pick up the trail we'll be miles away. Ye'll go with me, Radisson? Come, have sense, man! Of course ye don't know the Silent Ones—pray God you never will, for they're a fearsome sight! Don't make me use force on ye, to-night of all nights—but say ye'll go!"

Barr glanced around at the dark faces, and knew that whatever this weird greeting meant, there was, at least, the right of might behind the appeal. And on the instant something in the big man seemed to draw him—some lonely grip that reached out and conquered him in its wistfulness.

"I'll go," he said simply.

CHAPTER V

THE WHITE TOBACCO GIRL

"GOOD!"
Montenay turned with a sharp order. The dogs began to snarl in wild confusion, the loaded snake-whips trailed out their thirty-foot lashes and restored order, and a moment later the ten Chipewas, headed by Nichemus, took the trail. Montenay and Barr followed, side by side.

The American regretted his decision almost instantly, but it was too late now. Suddenly he turned to the other, remembering that shot across the snow.

"Was it by your orders that Nichemus fired on us and killed a dog, Montenay?"

"No, it was not on you that he fired, friend Radisson. He has borne a grudge against Uchichak for a long time."

"Well, a thing like that won't go unpunished—"

"Tut, tut!" Montenay interrupted with great good humor that nothing could shake. "Nothing but firewater can interfere with an Injun's feud, Radisson," for so he always used the name. "He saw his chance, and took it, which is Injun nature."

Barr fell silent for a little, his mind reverting to Montenay's earlier words. Why had the man feared his coming for a year past, and who were the Silent Ones? And what did "to-night of all nights" signify?

Where they were bound for he had not the slightest idea, nor could he imagine why Montenay was so evidently anxious to have his friendship. The whole affair was a tremendously vexing puzzle, with no solution in sight.

"Well, Mack will probably follow us," he thought, "and I guess he can take care of himself. Besides, Uchichak's men will be along before many days."

He had not been given his rifle, which Nichemus still carried, and he put a curt request for it to Montenay. The other slapped him on the shoulder with a laugh.

"Not yet; not yet! Have patience, man; if all goes well with us, we'll have a little talk with Pierre and arrange things satisfactorily. If ye like, I may hand over everything to you and skip out for the South—'twill depend on Minebegonequay. First, we'll have to see what Pierre has to say about it, though."

"Pierre who?"

"Pierre Radisson, of course."

Radison stared for a second, but Montenay seemed to think little of the words. "A little talk with Pierre"—and this particular Pierre dead for two hundred years! What Noreen Murphy had to do with it, troubled Barr little.

Yet if Montenay were crazy, it would not explain his evident power. The odd belt that he wore over his capote instead of sash, like some symbol of authority, the pelts, the flintlock pistol—the whole thing seemed to have some mystery behind it. Straightway Barr decided that Montenay was not crazy; he was an immense brute of a man, whose mind might be a trifle warped, but he was plainly of birth and breeding.

"Time will show," concluded the American with a little shrug of resignation. "I suppose we're going to get his sweetheart, as McShayne thought. I wonder what on earth ever got him started on this Pierre Radisson stuff?"

He recalled the story of the old explorer—how, deserted and betrayed on every hand, the man who had opened all the North and West to trade suddenly disappeared. Whether he had died in broken poverty; whether he had made his way back to his ancient friends the Mohawks; whether he had borne up once more for the great bay where he had raided and pirated and made his name a terror, no one ever knew. Pierre Radisson had vanished, though his sons had come to the Detroit with Cadillac.

However, he was not greatly concerned with a two-hundred-year-old Canadian just at present. He knew that the party was keeping to the northeast, plunging through the heavy timber that skirted the long and crooked Wusap Lake, though they did not debouch upon the lake itself. Once the lonely, terrible wolf-cry shrilled through the trees far to their right, and Montenay turned with a smile.

"The cry of the kill, Radisson! This is the seventh year, and the wolves are bad to meet with."

Barr nodded. "Yes, the rabbits were pretty scarce as we came north. You don't know what that seven-year business is, I suppose?"

"No, nor any one else. Every seventh year, as sure as fate itself, the rabbits die off and there's no trapping them. It's bad for the animals who live on 'em, too. A queer country."

"Aren't you a Scotchman?" inquired Radison, something in the deep voice giving him the idea. He half expected Montenay to flare up, but the giant was in a jovial mood and merely laughed rumblingly, as one would laugh to a child's question.

"Aye, like enough, but no man is the master of Macferris Montenay now, bear that in mind. What I've won I'll keep—here, try this."

He pulled a flask from inside his capote, where the heat of

his body kept the liquor from freezing, and passed it over. Radison was weary and cold, and unscrewing the cap he took a swallow of fiery liquid.

"Great Scott, man!" he gasped, handing it back quickly. "Where did you get such stuff as that? How old is it?"

"Ask the Silent Ones," gurgled Montenay. The drink seemed to change his mood abruptly, for he shot a dark glance at the American. "Don't get too curious, Radisson—it don't set well on a man o' your name."

The warning was enough, though Barr had never tasted such liquor as that in all his life. Warmed and heartened by the few drops he had swallowed, he plodded ahead with new energy.

It irritated him that Montenay persistently stuck to the French form of his name, but he kept his thoughts to himself, for a word seemed to set the giant off when liquor was in him.

A wild conjecture flitted through his brain—a thought that Montenay might, after all, have established a rude kingdom here in the Empty Places where no man was lord, that he might have brought the Chipewas under his rule by dint of religious frenzy, that he might have formed a confederacy which in future would cause trouble, as Macklin had guessed.

But the thought was too wild, too improbable. Neither Montenay nor any other man could do such a thing without the news being borne to the outer world, Barr knew well enough.

Suddenly the string of men ahead halted in a clump of spruce, and a little fire was built. While Nichemus was making tea, Radison flung himself down on one of the dog-sleds, which was empty save for a few furs, and stretched out to rest.

Montenay talked with his followers in their own tongue, and the American noticed that all carried muskets, while the giant himself bore a rifle. Whatever the purpose of the expedition was, it hardly seemed a wedding-party, he thought.

A cup of tea and some half-thawed pemmican was eaten in silence, Radison, receiving no less and no more than the rest, including Montenay himself. Since there seemed to be a good store of provision on the loaded sled, this careful portioning out the rations foreboded a long and hard trip ahead, it appeared.

A swift order from Montenay and all the men save Nichemus leaped up and got into their snowshoes, took their rifles and, without a word, filed off. Montenay turned to the startled Radison, who wondered what this new move meant.

"We'll be back in an hour, friend Nichemus will stay to keep ye company—eh, Jean?"

The breed, it seemed, was also a person of moods, for he flashed one sullen glance at Montenay and went on with his work of scraping the frost-rime from his capote. Before Radison could speak, the giant caught up his own rifle and was gone on the trail of the rest.

"Where are they off to, Nichemus?" queried the American.

Slowly the breed looked up and met his eyes. The thin, sensitive face was hard and set, and the eyes were wholly brutal now.

"To raise de hell, m'sieu. I t'ink me some one die, to-night."

"Well, I guess they're the ones can raise considerable Cain," and Radison got out his pipe, lighting it from an ember. "A pipe certainly does taste good when you light it from a fire!" he sighed contentedly. "By the way, where are we? Anywhere near Murphy's post?"

"Huh? How you know 'bout heem?"

The Indian was certainly uppermost in Jean Nichemus now, thought the other, as he noted the lowering, vindictive gaze of the man.

"Oh, I heard about it! Are we near the place?"

For answer Nichemus picked up his rifle, carried a brand twenty feet away, coolly built himself another fire, and settled down to watch. Radison flushed angrily at the action, then stretched out on his sled and fixed his eyes on the huskies. After the manner of their kind they lay motionless, asleep; but let him move a hand and every sharp eye would open the merest trifle.

There was silence for half an hour, and Barr was just dozing comfortably when a single sharp rifle-shot sounded clear and distinct, though from some distance. He sat up, startled, to see Nichemus on his feet.

"What was that—some one hunting?"

"Be quiet!" The breed turned a face on him that was like a snarling wolf's, and Radison was wide awake instantly. "He's be de king's wife, mebbe; we see ver' soon."

The king's wife! Was it possible that anything so romantic as an elopement was going on here amid the snows? Barr tried to picture Montenay making love, and chuckled. There was something wistful about the fellow, at times, but certainly nothing of the lover.

"Look here, Nichemus," he said good humoredly, "you aren't going to keep me from talking, anyhow. I suppose your friend the king is running off with the girl called Minebegonequay, isn't he? Loosen up, old man!"

Nichemus quietly strode over, his face working with passion, and faced Barr.

"Listen! By Goss, I say for be quiet, you be *quiet!* De debil he is raise' in me dis night, *m'sieu*—an' I t'ink I la'k for keel you w'en you make for talk!"

The hoarse words issued like a growl from the man, but Radison, still seated, laughed and stretched forth a hand.

"Give me your fist."

For an instant the other hesitated, then shifted his rifle and obeyed. Barr put all his force into the grip, and rose swiftly to his feet as Nichemus doubled up in pain. Kicking away the rifle, he caught the breed by the throat and bent him back across the dog-sled. So swiftly was it all done that before the rifle lay quiet on the snow, Barr was staring down into the distorted eyes, his weight holding Nichemus firmly against the sled.

"You fool!" he said slowly, grimly. "Do you think you can

order me around like that? Talk of killing me—you! You raise all the devil you want to and I'll choke it out of you in mighty short order, Jean Nichemus! Now, get up and behave yourself."

He jerked the breed to his feet, half thinking to see the long knife flash out; but to his surprise Nichemus stood feeling his hand, a ghastly smile flitting across his face, his dark eyes looking steadily at Radison.

"M'sieu, s'pose dere be jus' one star on de sky, an' de night, she's be all de time; jus' dat one *petite* star, no more. Den s'pose God, he's put out his han' for take dat star an' make it dark—eh? Mebbe de debil he's be raise' in you, too."

He turned away abruptly, picked up his rifle, and crouched down by his fire. As Radison watched him, thinking that he understood, a flash of pity came into his heart.

"Poor devil!" he thought to himself. "I suppose this bunch brought him some bad news—his squaw dead, or something like that. I'll swear there was no fear in his eyes, though! Poor devil!"

He stared at the huddled figure reflectively, for there was a queer Latin strain in some of these French half-breeds, a strain that seemed oddly out of place here in the northland. Suddenly Barr turned with a start; a dark shadow was slipping through the trees, and even as Nichemus gained his feet one of the Chipewas ran up and tied on his snowshoes.

Then came another and another, all panting hard. Radison counted nine, then he felt his heart leap as the great form of Montenay loomed up, doubly huge. Over the giant's shoulder was flung a figure thickly wrapped in furs; he lowered it to the empty sled beside Radison, but no sign of life came from it. The American looked about for the tenth Chipewa—and then he saw that one of the men carried two guns.

"Where's your other man?" he inquired lightly. "Have a scrap?"

He started again, as Montenay looked up. The man's face was

lit with a strange passion, and the black beard was stiff with frozen blood, lightly covered with white frost-rime.

"Aye, a bit of a scrap, Radison. Get your shoes on, man."

He obeyed without a murmur. The huskies were beaten into snarling submission and were quickly harnessed, then Nichemus swung away to break the trail, Montenay snapped out a deep *"Mash! Mash!"* and the march was on.

With mind awhirl Radison fell into line behind the giant; what was the meaning of this rapid march, this silent figure on the sled? Was it the tenth Chipewa, and had Montenay been foiled in his elopement?

But soon the American was too spent for wonder. He began to realize that he had hardly slept since leaving the fort, and the pace set by Nichemus was a cruel one; the monotonous thrust of the snowshoes was terrible, but he gave no sign of weakness, only clenching his teeth grimly with the determination to keep going until he dropped. He wished now that he had slept while alone with the breed.

The swift march continued only an hour, however. Then Montenay rasped out a growling order and the band halted, Nichemus stripping some bark and starting a fire.

Radison dropped in his tracks, but as he saw Montenay approach the sled his curiosity was greater than his weariness, and he pulled himself up on one elbow, watching. The giant threw off the bands of hide and pulled up the bundle of furs; an instant later Barr heard a startled cry as a face emerged from the furs.

Transfixed, he gazed as it lay on Montenay's arm—pale, with deep golden-red hair drifting out over the dark furs like lost strands of sunlight. Then the violet eyes met his, and their horror-struck look brought him to his feet, tired as he was.

Instantly he realized the whole thing. This was no elopement; this girl was no willing bride—but a captive, taken in primal fashion by this giant of the snows!

As he gained his feet he saw the violet eyes fixed on him in startled appeal. Beyond that first low cry, the girl had made no sound. Radison sprang to Montenay's side, not heeding Niche-mus, who drew close at the movement.

"What is this deviltry?" he cried hoarsely, tugging at the giant's shoulder. The bearded, blood-flecked face was slowly upturned to his. "Who is this girl, Montenay?"

"My wife to be, so mind your own affairs," came the amazing response. Startled, Barr stared down at the pale face among the furs, but at the words it had flashed into a quick blaze of protest.

"No!" came the cry, as the girl's hands struck out to push Montenay away. "They stole into the house last night. Help me, help me!"

Radison forgot his weariness in a wild flame of rage, and with one quick snarl he sprang at Montenay. As he struck at the scowling face a foot tripped him and he rolled headlong; a dozen hands gripped and struck at him, but he broke free with one savage effort.

Gaining his knees, he sent blow after blow against the lithe, dark bodies which had hemmed him in. Fingers clutched at his neck, but he tore them away, struggling to his feet, silent in the grasp of the terrible battle-lust that was on him. Men were on his back, clinging to his arms and legs and shoulders, but still he dragged them slowly forward, every energy centered on reaching that scowling face above the sled.

One brave after another went down, reeling, staggering back before him; his fist crashed into the face of the Chipewa who clung to his knees; a kick freed him from another; and there, only a step ahead, was Montenay, who had risen to his feet in amazement at the struggle.

The fury was full on Radison now. He lunged forward with a yell of exultation and struck with his whole weight, his fist crashing into the tangle of blood-frozen beard.

He saw Montenay waver and go back, felt the great hands grip him as if they would crush shoulders and ribs together, and his fist thudded home again.

The grip loosened, and he felt a fierce delight at sight of his own torn, bleeding knuckles; then the sky seemed to fall on him and all things went from red to black.

Nichemus stood ready for a second stroke with his rifle clubbed, but there was no need, and Montenay regained his feet in time to hold him back. The pale face of the girl was once more buried among the dark furs, and for a space only the cracking whips and yelpings echoed through the trees, as the excited dogs were beaten into quiet.

Montenay stood over the American with a grim smile, then he rolled the body on its back and gazed down at the deadly pale features, on which the blood was already frozen. Suddenly he went to his knees, flung back the hood from Radison's head, and called Nichemus, while the others made camp.

Here the band rested two hours, and although Montenay attempted to revive Radison, the American remained as if dead. Finally he was tied on the sled which carried the provisions; Nichemus cracked his whip, and the dogs moved off to the east, followed by the Chipewas.

Behind, and a quarter-mile to one side, among the bushes on a hill, Macklin snapped his glasses together and turned to his companion.

"Whew! That was some fight Rad put up, chief! Who was the girl on the sled?"

The other nodded, his deep-set eyes burning.

"Napawew! He is a man! The girl is the white tobacco girl, my brother—Minebegonequay. Let us go to the small master's house and wait for news of my young men."

And save for the snakelike file of men that crept away to the northeast, the Empty Places were silent and deserted, while around the horizon hovered the sundogs, boding storm.

CHAPTER VI

IN THE GHOST HILLS

STRANGE DREAMS came to Barr Radison—brief, fitful memories of things that occurred at intervals, yet all a grotesque jumble of dream-fancies. There was a confused recollection of sun and storm, of black sky and weird Spirit Dancers above him, of hands that cared for and fed him, and of tears that dropped on his face to arouse him.

At times soft fingers would rest on his brow and a pale, violet-eyed face would enter his dream; at times the rough beard of Montenay would sweep his face and rough hands touch his head until the pain of it brought blackness upon him. And above all were the lights, endless, changeless, and yet ever changing, in flicker of light and shadow.

Suddenly the dream became a nightmare, vague and horrible, and this was the fashion of it.

All about were hills, purpled in the unearthly glare of the dancers, slowly drawing nearer and closing in. They seemed to break straight out of the ground—masses of black rock that stood out bare and bleak, until the trail wound between gaunt walls that shut out even the fires in the heavens, and then plunged downward, while a bitter wind bit them to the marrow.

Then it seemed to Radison that he was swallowed up in a terrible abyss of rock and snow, the weirdness of the place even moving the huskies to strange whines of fear.

All was silent save for the howl of the wind, that shot down through those pits of darkness until he seemed to see men staggering and reeling before it, while icy particles of snow drove into him like tiny knives, invisible until they stung and burned.

As they drew deeper and deeper into the blackness, queer moaning echoes were sent flying by wind and voices and sled-creaks; they were not borne past, but eddied up and up as though some flux of the wind caught and whirled them back.

Then the dream took new form, and it appeared as if he stood on the brink of great crags and gazed off across illimitable distances of snow and bare black rock; and all died away once more into the depths of unconsciousness.

When finally Radison came to himself he was lying in darkness, a heavy weight upon him. Putting out his hards, he felt that the weight was a fur-skin, but he could not move it, and realized that he must be strangely weak. Suddenly the darkness was rent apart, and he lay staring, fearing that this must be part of his dream, nor daring to move lest it vanish with the rest.

Standing in the doorway, holding the skin-flap open, stood the girl of the sled. To one side of her a fire was sputtering with birch-bark, and Radison saw that he lay in a rude log hut of two rooms, furs and pelts all about him. It was not at this he looked, however, but at the girl in the doorway, who was steadily watching his recumbent form.

Very beautiful she seemed, there in the soft birch-glow, which tinged her golden hair with ruddy hues and livened her grave, sweet face with the rise and fall of the flames.

She wore no furs, and her inner dress of doe-skin, decorated with the beautifully marked neck-skins of loons, betrayed every line and curve of her slender, almost girlish figure.

Yet there was little else of the girl about her, as Radison could see. Brow, eyes, and mouth revealed the woman, for in this half shadow each line of the features stood out in bold relief. Radison guessed that she was twenty, or perhaps a little over.

"I wish you'd take off this robe," he said, but his voice sounded husky and faint in his ears.

"Mr. Radisson!" came a soft, hesitant voice, and the girl approached. "Are you conscious?"

"Also thirsty," he rejoined, with an attempt at a laugh. "A drink would—"

"Thank God!" she broke in, a little sob in her throat. "I feared that you were—were raving again."

She knelt at his side, a hand stole under his head, and with unutterable relief he drank long of the cool water she gave him, sinking back with a sigh.

"Fine! So I've been off my head, eh? Are you the girl—the girl on the sled?"

"Yes; but don't try to talk now, Mr. Radisson. You've been very ill, and—"

"And you've been taking care of me?" finished Barr. "But please don't call me Radisson—it reminds me of Montenay and gets on my nerves."

"Very well," she returned soothingly. "Please don't try to talk now."

"But I want to, and I'm going to," he smiled quickly. "Tell me who you are."

"I'm Noreen Murphy, and my father's the free trader at Wusap Lake. Do be satisfied with that and go to sleep, for you need it badly. Next time you wake up I'll tell you all you want to know—and there are some things for you to tell me, too."

"Is that a promise?" queried Barr, drowsy already, in spite of his curiosity.

"It's a promise, so go to sleep like a good boy."

"Not any more—forgot to be a boy long time ago," he muttered thickly. "Anyway, now I know why—they call you—Minebegonequay."

And with that word he fell asleep, still dreaming of the hair that glowed in the ruddy flare like the golden buttercup flowers that glow in the snow-wastes of the north. Girl-who-wears-flowers-in-her-hair! The word, borrowed by these people of the Empty Places from their Saulteaux neighbors in the south, was strangely fanciful and strangely beautiful withal.

When next Radison awoke the firelight was streaming into his room, and by its glow he perceived the huge form of Montenay seated on the skins beside him, while Noreen was standing in the doorway.

"Awake, are ye?" rumbled the giant, and Barr felt a rough but tender hand smoothing back his hair. The deep voice sounded again, and it was softened oddly. "Man, why would ye not be friends with me? Here, drink this caribou broth."

Too weak to argue, Radison obeyed, and the hot, meaty drink gave him new life. He pushed away the great hand impatiently as it wandered back to his brow.

"Keep your hands off me! Take that girl back to her home, Montenay, or I'll see you punished for your dirty work yet."

"What a devil for fight the man is!" Montenay grinned complacently. "As for Noreen—tut, tut! Why, I have loved the girl for years, Radisson; loved her when she used to sit on my knee and pull my beard—loved her when Père Sulvent sneaked her off to school in Quebec—loved her when—"

"But she doesn't love you!" flashed out the girl suddenly from the doorway. "And I'll never marry you, Mad Montenay!"

At the last words Barr heard the giant catch his breath swiftly.

"Mad is it?" he repeated slowly. "Yet ye'll marry me right soon, Noreen dear! Oh, Minebegonequay! It'll be a dark day for you if ever ye drive Macferris Montenay mad in truth!"

Abruptly, Montenay rose and left the place. Radison tried to move, but desisted with a groan, for his head throbbed with pain. He felt, rather than saw, the girl cross swiftly to him, and as something splashed in his neck he put up a hand that caught hers blindly.

"There, there," he exclaimed, "cheer up, Noreen! I'll soon be on my feet again, and then we'll see what we can do. Now, I wish you'd relieve my curiosity; there are about a million things I want to know."

"But you aren't strong enough to talk," she protested, gently removing her hand. Barr liked her the more for the little action.

"Of course I am," he persisted, smiling. "At least my body may be weak, but my head's clear as a bell. Let's see—first, how long have I been knocked out? As I remember, it came just after I landed on Montenay."

"Yes—Jean Nichemus hit you with his rifle. Oh, I was so afraid you were dead! You've been ill for more than two weeks; we reached here four days ago, and you've been talking wildly all the time."

"H-m!" reflected Barr, somewhat startled. "Haven't been saying naughty things, have I?"

"That depends." Her light laugh floated down to him. "I don't think you need worry, though. You were only shocking when Mad Montenay was around."

"Mad Montenay, eh? Pretty good name. Tell me, Noreen, did we come through some terrible hills? I thought maybe I dreamed it."

"Yes—the Ghost Hills they called them. We had heard of them often, but I never thought such a horrible place really existed. Truly, I didn't mean to call him that name; but it's one father always used for him, and it just—slipped out.

"Now, it's your turn, if you please; Montenay calls you Radisson, but you said that wasn't your name, so I don't know quite who you *are*."

Laughing, Barr explained the delusion under which the giant seemed to labor in regard to his name, nor could the girl throw any light upon it. He went on to tell her of his mission in this wilderness, and remembered Macklin—also the fact that as yet he knew nothing of the girl's story.

"I have seen nothing of your friend," she replied to his eager questions, "though I have heard father mention his name. Why, you seem to know more of my capture than I do.

"I woke up in the night and heard a shot; then some one ran into my room—it must have been Montenay himself—and bundled me all up in furs. I tried to fight against him and to call father, but I must have fainted for I don't remember anything more till that terrible fight there by the sleds. Now, I think you've talked enough, Mr. Radison—"

"Make it Barr, and I'll drop right off," he broke in, smiling. "Anyway, I'm going to call you Noreen, because it seems to fit pretty well."

"All right—Barr," she laughed softly. "Now go to sleep!"

He did so, readily enough. His wound had begun to throb anew, and the need for rest was strong upon him. Thus passed two more days, between eating and talking and sleeping, while sometimes Noreen was with him, sometimes Montenay.

Always the big man was as tender as the girl, as gentle and considerate of everything, for Barr was careful not to excite him, and he seemed to keep free of liquor. During those two days Radison mended fast, and on the third day the American was able to wrap himself in furs and leave the shack for some fresh air.

His first view of the place was astonishing enough. The log shack, with one or two more, lay at the edge of a great deserted village. In every direction stretched the bare poplar and willow uprights, and over half a dozen of these were stretched deerskin; in these lodges dwelt the few Chipewas who had accompanied Montenay, the rest of the Indians being out on their hunting grounds.

Beyond the village, on one side, stretched a rolling, tree-scattered wilderness, but on the other, a scant half-mile distant, lay those terrible hills of which he had dreamed. Now, he saw that the dream was reality, and as he gazed at the wind-swept masses of bleak rock he whistled in dismay at their bleak appearance.

"Whew! Where did we ever get through there, Noreen?"

The girl at his side flushed slightly at the name, but pointed with a smile to a dark cleft, almost directly opposite. The ground between rose in long swells, and was dotted with willows, interspersed with poplars and bushes; but Radison could clearly make out the black notch in those iron cliffs, as she followed the pointing finger.

"There it is, Barr. Ugh! I never saw such a terrible place—the trail seemed to go down and down, until the rocks shut out all light! The wind whistled through that narrow cañon as if—"

"I remember that well enough!" he exclaimed, gazing at the hills which hemmed in the village on the west and south. "It's easy to see why they're called Ghost Hills, all right. By the way, where's Nichemus? I haven't seen him around."

"I don't know—he went off three days ago and hasn't come back. Here's Talking Owl—he and Yellow Wolf, over there, seem to be in charge, when Montenay is gone."

A short but powerfully-built warrior stalked past, apparently taking no notice of the two figures outside the shack, and Radison saw Yellow Wolf bending over a fire near-by. The latter warrior wore a peculiar cap formed from a wolf's head, one ear of which was missing. Noreen smiled slightly as her eyes followed Talking Owl.

"What children they are! That chief has visited us a hundred times, yet he won't pay any attention to me because I'm a woman!"

"They're rather dangerous children to be out of school," chuckled Radison. "But tell me what you know about this man Montenay. He seems to have known you all your life, from what he said the other day."

It was a strange story that the girl told him, as they slowly walked through the village and watched the Chipewas drying caribou meat in the smoke of their lodges.

Years before, John Murphy had made a home for himself at Wusap Lake, setting up as an independent trader. He had soon gained the Chipewas over to deal with him, and had finally brought his young wife up from the south.

When Noreen came, she had died, and father and daughter had never been separated until Père Sulvent induced Murphy to send the girl to school at Quebec.

"Montenay was very angry about it, I remember," she said. "It was only six months ago that poor Père Sulvent went out and never returned. I wouldn't be surprised if Montenay knew what had become of him, either, for he had threatened the good father several times.

"He used to hang about our post a good deal, but I never suspected that—that he was in love with me, nor did father. He gave me a wonderful coat of black fox once, and often brought in some to trade—"

"Ah!" broke in Radison quickly. "That's what Macklin and I came up here to find out about, as I told you—or rather, Macklin brought me along with him. Have you any idea as to where Montenay got the skins?"

"No, and father used to wonder about it a good deal, though he never asked any direct questions. The last time Montenay came to the house was a month ago, and he was in such a condition that father ordered him off the place.

"A week later Nichemus came and dropped a few vague hints of trouble, but we could get nothing out of him. Jean has visited us quite often within the last year, and I never thought he would take part in such an outrage."

"Poor devil, I guess he has troubles of his own!" returned Radison. "Well, I have a whole lot of confidence in Macklin and Uchichak, but I don't think they'll ever get through those hills, from what I remember of the way we came. If we're to get out of this it'll have to be done on our own hook—and I'm in no shape to travel just yet."

"Oh, it's terrible—terrible!" broke out the girl hopelessly, gazing across the barrens that stretched to the desolate north. "We could never get away from here without help, Barr."

"Well, we aren't going to hang around and do nothing, you can bet on that," answered the American confidently. "You just wait till I get some strength into my legs, and it'll be a funny thing if I don't make Montenay do some tall hustling! What's that sheen along the horizon to the east?"

Noreen turned and gazed at the skyline, where there hung a slight glimmer as if the sun were reflected from some polished surface.

"It must be the ice-glint," she responded slowly. "I suppose we are near the bay. We can be thankful that the darkness is over, for I could stand the all-year winter, but if we were shut up here with the long night just beginning it would be horrible. Now come back to the shack, Barr; you've done quite enough for to-day."

As Radison was of that opinion himself, he obeyed meekly. Through the days that followed he devoted himself to regaining strength, and inside of a week was almost himself again; for there was no lack of fresh meat, caribou being abundant and even one or two moose being brought into camp.

He saw little of Montenay during that time. As soon as he was able to be on his feet and out of Noreen's care Talking Owl assigned him to one of the lodges. The large shack was used as a storehouse for pelts, Montenay occupied the second, and the smallest was fitted up for Noreen.

One morning, however, as he stood talking with Noreen, Montenay appeared in the door of his shack and called him. The giant motioned the girl back as she started to accompany Barr.

"No, I want you alone, Radisson. I'm thinking that it's time we had a little talk."

"So am I," returned Barr grimly, and, with a reassuring word to the girl, he strode over to the shack and entered.

CHAPTER VII

BEYOND THE LAW

LIKE EVERYTHING connected with Montenay, his shack was peculiar unto itself. Radison stepped into the pungent odor of old pelts, and saw half a dozen bundles of skins piled in a corner near Montenay's home-made couch. But it was at the walls that he looked, for the shack was a veritable arsenal.

The repeating rifles and a heavy-bore shotgun lay across the wide antlers of a moose head, and hanging from a pair of caribou horns were three more cased weapons.

On a shelf formed by a log protruding inward lay an old flintlock musket, hunting knives and hatchets were thrust in chinks of the logs, and boxes of ammunition stood all about, From one of the moose antlers hung that long belt of odd beads which Montenay had worn at the post, and beside it was a long, curved powder-horn from which depended tassels of the same curious beads.

The American made himself comfortable on the couch beside the little box stove, flung open his capote, pulled out his pipe, and waited for Montenay to begin the conversation. This the other was not long in doing, in his customary surprising fashion.

"Radisson, ye remember that night at the post when ye spoiled my luck? I wish ye'd teach me that tune; the words go fine to it!"

This was too much for Barr, and he broke into a laugh.

"Montenay, you've sure got my goat! Where on earth did you get those words? Did the Silent Ones—"

"Ye're a good guesser, Radisson!" broke in the giant, with a dark glance. "Now, will ye do it or not?"

Willing to humor him, Barr whistled the tune over and over, while Montenay, his face set in earnest effort, fitted the words to the air until he caught the lilt of it and began to roar it out like a delighted child with a new toy. Finally Barr tired of it, however, and determined to get the giant back to realities.

"Ye'd better practise that off among the Ghost Hills by yourself," he laughed. "Let's get down to business, Montenay. I'll take it for granted that you're serious in this abduction of Miss Murphy; but you ought to know as well as I do that it can't end this way. Murphy will be after you, to say nothing of Macklin and—"

"Tut, tut! Your friends could never pass through these same Ghost Hills, man! And as for Murphy, he's buried by now!"

"What! Is he dead?" Radison stared through the blue tobacco-smoke.

"Aye. The fool shot Yellow Wolf's brother that night, and the men finished him. However, 'tis all for the best, Barr. Had he lived he might have made trouble, and now Noreen and I can marry in peace."

"Marry? Who'll marry you? Does she know about her father?"

"Not yet. As for the ceremony, that will be held Chipewa fashion, with a white man's wedding to boot. Oh, it's all fixed, Radisson; some of the squaws will be in to-morrow, and the hunters will come in before long."

Despite his anger, Barr mastered the impulse to spring at Montenay. Even should he master the giant, which was doubtful considering his present condition, the braves in the village would soon overpower him. No; it would be better to wait—to bide his time and strike when success seemed at least possible.

"Well, I'm glad you're so sure of yourself," he replied dryly. "What priest will you get—the ghost of Père Sulvent, maybe?"

Montenay started as if stung, darted one flame-filled glance at Barr, then leaned back with a low laugh.

"So you've heard o' that, eh? Ye'll be surprised when ye see the priest, Radisson!" He chuckled to himself for a moment. "No, Sulvent is dead as Murphy, rest his soul! Now, I'd like to know just where we stand, Barr. We might as well be friends— and I need ye bad, man!

"Frankly, I'm holding these Chipewas by main force. If they weren't feared o' me an' worse feared o' the Silent Ones, they'd be on my back in no time. Jean Nichemus and Talking Owl are the only ones I can trust. Oh, they'd fight for me, never fear; but with the lash over 'em. Join with me, Radisson, and we'll do big things!"

This time the appeal did not move Barr, and he merely puffed at his pipe, eying Montenay coolly and reflectively.

"No use, Macferris Montenay," he returned at length. "I don't know what all your talk about Pierre Radisson and the Silent Ones may mean, and I don't give two whoops in purgatory. You've stolen Noreen Murphy, and you can't talk business with me until she has been taken home, so you might as well quit trying.

"And I'll give you fair warning that if you try any tricks while I'm around you'll be sorry for it. I'm not dead, by a long shot, and while there are some things I like about you, I think you'll regret yet that you didn't finish me off while you had a chance.

"You've raised the limit to the roof in this deal, and unless you back down mighty sudden I'll take off the roof and wade in. That's all I have to say on the subject."

The giant gazed at him, nodding as to some unspoken thought. Then he leaned forward, that strange touch of wistfulness in his face once more.

"I'm sorry, Radisson. Twice now have I kept my hands off you, for the love I felt toward you, and ye have repaid me poorly. I'd do anything in God's world to win ye over, man, except the thing you ask. I won't give up Minebegonequay for man, God, or devil; so put that in your pipe, my lad!

"It's brave talk ye make, Barr Radisson, but talk will do ye no good; so give over such madness. Go out—run away if ye want to! Take a pair of snow-shoes—there's plenty leaning against the ledges—and try to get away. Where would ye go? Even with dogs you could never find your way back to Tenacity; so let be. Think it over—there's no hurry—and if ye change your mind just drop me a nod and we'll have a talk with Pierre."

"Damn Pierre—and you, too!" exclaimed Barr, exasperated, as he rose and stalked out of the shack. Who or what was this mysterious Pierre and the still more mysterious Silent Ones? The rumbling laugh of Montenay only exasperated him further, and after assuring the rather alarmed Noreen that he had received no harm, he proceeded to test the sincerity of the giant's words by taking her for a walk out of the village toward the cliffs.

To his surprise, no one interfered with them, nor did any of the Chipewas follow after; but the farther they went the more disgusted was Barr with the lonely hills and desolation on all sides. It was not long before they returned to the village, passing Montenay on the way; and Noreen paid no heed to his word of greeting, but marched past with her head in the air, Barr catching a rueful wink from the giant.

The next morning all the braves except Talking Owl departed for a great hunt, and Radison gathered that a large number of Chipewas were expected soon. That afternoon he was talking to Noreen at the door of her shack, when she uttered a low cry and caught at his arm.

"Look! He's been drinking again, and he's coming here!"

Barr whirled and saw Montenay lurching over the snow toward them, an evil light in his dark face, and knew that the drink-demon had entered into the man.

In spite of the situation, however, a little thrill ran through him as he turned and caught the hand that lay on his arm.

Gently but firmly he pushed the girl inside the shack, which boasted a rude door of adz-hewn logs.

"Shut the door, Noreen, and don't open to him. I'll try and hold him if he makes trouble."

"You mustn't—you aren't strong enough!" she cried quickly; but he merely smiled, overruled her protest by closing the door, and turned to meet Montenay, who seemed wild with rage at the action.

"So—shut the door in my face, will ye? Who's master here but King Montenay?"

"King Whisky," retorted Radison bitterly.

To his surprise, the other stood swaying for a moment; then his face cleared.

Putting out both his long arms, he gripped Barr by the shoulders, and, with a grin, lifted him clear of the ground as he might have raised a child.

"Could ye do that with *me,* man? But Montenay's luck is more than all his strength; so give us the tune and I'll set ye down in peace."

"Put me down, you idiot, or I'll wipe that grin off your face!" cried Barr, raging in impotent wrath.

Montenay obeyed without a protest, merely repeating his request for "the tune," and the angry Barr restrained himself enough to whistle the old pirate air, whereupon Montenay caught the swing of it and lurched away with a swagger, roaring out, "Down among the dead men—let—him—*lie!*" at the top of his voice.

Sorely puzzled, Radison watched him reel off over the snow—and a sudden startling idea leaped into his mind. A swift glance showed him that Talking Owl was not in sight, and without an instant's hesitation he plunged forward among the bare lodge-poles, following that roaring bass voice.

For Montenay had started, not toward his own shack, but directly out of the village toward the hills; and it had occurred to the American that this might be a chance to solve some of the vexing problems of the place, as he had no doubt that Montenay was returning to his liquor supply, wherever that might be.

Reaching the edge of the village, he made out the tall form of Montenay vanishing among the scattered poplars and willows of the hillside beyond.

Waiting until the giant was well out of sight, he plunged across the open space, floundering to his knees in the snow, and a moment later he had gained the cover of the trees. There was no sign of Talking Owl behind, and he decided that luck must have favored him in getting away unseen.

Up the long slope he struggled, warily keeping out of sight of the man ahead; for although Montenay seemed comfortably drunk, Barr noted that he was certainly walking straight. Soon the trees thinned out, and ahead rose the abrupt line of cliffs, with a space of bleak, wind-swept rock between.

Radison watched Montenay stagger out, and suddenly realized that directly before him was that V-like notch in the cliffs through which they had come to the village!

Biting his lip impatiently, he saw the giant approach the narrow black cleft above, and he dared not leave the cover of the trees until the other had gone on. It was well that he did not; for Montenay paused, drew himself up, and took a long look around before he vanished over the lip of rock.

Radison crossed the open stretch at a run, and as he came to the notch a furious wind smote him and sent him staggering. Standing there on the crest, with the crags on either hand, he saw that this wind must be eternally blowing down into and through that narrow, cañonlike opening, which led down into blackness beyond him and twisted out of sight. To his surprise, there was no sign of Montenay in sight.

That the giant could have passed on down the trail was incredible, for the first twist was a hundred yards ahead, and Barr must surely have seen him. Then the American looked at the trail, but the snow in the narrow cleft was hard and firm, and no trace of footprint met his eye.

"Well, this certainly has me beaten," he thought wonderingly. "He might have a cave or shack somewhere along in here, but I guess I won't take any chances. I've found out something, and it wouldn't pay to risk it."

Retreating to the trees, he looked along the line of cliffs. At points these seemed to be broken, with small hills adjoining the basin which stretched away to the north, and as he gazed Barr's face lit up,

"If I only had a pair of field-glasses here! I'll bet a dollar that's a good-sized break over there—and there's not a soul in camp! By thunder, I believe it could be done, and if she's willing—"

He turned abruptly and began to follow his trail back to the village, excitement spurring him forward. Montenay drunk, probably gone for the night—every brave except Talking Owl off on the hunt—Montenay's dogs and sled here—What better opportunity would ever present itself for escape?

Half fearing that he had deceived himself on the all-important question of the dogs, Barr flung a look around as he reached the village. No; there were one or two of the huskies in the doorway of the lodge they occupied—a moss-chinked, mud-banked lodge of split poles, lacking only the skins to make it cold-proof, with smoke curling up from the three protruding poles at the top.

The door of Noreen's shack was still closed, but it was to the larger cabin of Montenay that Radison turned, with swift decision, for Talking Owl was no doubt in his own lodge a hundred yards away. Reaching the door of the shack, Radison found it closed, but not locked; for the giant had small need to fear theft from these men of his. The next moment Radison stepped inside.

A cry of satisfaction broke from him as he took down a rifle from the moose horns and turned to the cartridge-boxes. Filling the magazine and his pockets with cartridges, he turned and left the shack, striding toward Talking Owl's lodge. The flap of caribou hide was in place, and without hesitation Barr raised the weight of wood at the bottom and entered.

Talking Owl was seated on the farther side of the mud fire-place, working on a snow-shoe.

At sight of Radison he scowled, and his hand went down to his rifle beside him; but Barr covered him quickly.

"Put your hands up, Talking Owl!"

The Chipewa obeyed promptly, with a slight grin.

"How you t'ink get away, Strong Eyes, huh?"

"That's my affair, and I'm quite capable of handling it, my friend. Now, understand that I'm perfectly willing to put a bullet through you, chief or no chief, so don't try any fooling! Get up."

Talking Owl had a slight struggle, for he was sitting cross-legged and his hands were reaching for the lodge-poles.

Radison grinned.

"Pretty good, chief. Now, just circle around me and go out the door first. I'll bring you back pretty soon, unless you try some funny work and die suddenly."

The Chipewa grunted sarcastically, obeying the command in as dignified a manner as he could summon up. Out of compassion Barr flung up the hood of the man's capote as he passed, for the cold was bitter outside the lodge, and received a swift look of thanks.

"You starve, freeze to deat'," grunted Talking Owl as he stepped out. "Meet my young men, plenty bad."

"It'll be plenty bad for them if I do," rejoined Radison grimly. "Go to the shack of Minebegonequay and knock on the door."

He followed, keeping a wary eye on the chief, but the latter obeyed without protest. At the knock Noreen opened the door and stepped out.

Her eyes opened wide in astonishment at sight of the two men.

"What—where is Montenay?" she exclaimed.

Barr smiled.

"In the hills somewhere—dead to the world by this time, I hope. I'll have to ask you to let Talking Owl inside before his hands freeze—they're beginning to look white already."

She stepped aside, and the Chipewa entered without delay, Radison behind him.

The interior of Noreen's dwelling was decorated with pines; blankets, fur, and beadwork were on the walls; and Barr concluded that Montenay had prepared long in advance for his raid.

There was no time to waste, however, and, catching sight of some old snow-shoe thongs in the corner, he nodded toward them.

"Tie up his wrists, Noreen."

With a smile on his grim mouth, Talking Owl put out his hands and looked unwinkingly in the girl's face while she worked. Radison put down the rifle, motioned the chief to the couch, and tied his ankles securely.

"Now, slip on your mittens and come outside, Noreen. I'll explain there, where our friend won't embarrass us."

"What is it, Barr?" asked the girl anxiously, when they had left the shack.

Radison turned to her and met her level-eyed gaze, his eyes narrowing in a smile.

"We're going to strike for Tenacity, you and I," he returned quietly. "That is, if you're willing to chance it. Are you?"

CHAPTER VIII

ESCAPE

THE VIOLET eyes met his steadily as he described his pursuit of Montenay, and when he had concluded with a brief summary of the situation one little mittened hand went out to his and the girl's voice rang clear and strong: "Thank God that you are here, Mr.—Barr! If it hadn't been for you I don't know what would have happened by this time. Yes, of course we'll go!"

"You realize what it will mean," he returned gravely, searching her face as he spoke. "If it took us two weeks to get here, with plenty of everything, and with men who knew the way, we're apt to take a good deal longer getting out—to say nothing of getting lost. We'll have to keep ahead of pursuit; for I don't take any stock in Montenay's profession of security and his permission to wander about. And if we go we'll have to start inside of an hour and travel all night."

"I'm ready," she said simply; "but I don't think we could face that dreadful road through the hills. You can't imagine how terrible it was, even with a large party."

"Oh, I got a general impression—quite enough, too," laughed Radison. He turned the girl about and pointed toward the west. "There seems to be a break in the hills over there, about ten miles off, Noreen. I think we'd better head for that; and if we should get lost there are caribou herds within reach. No use chancing it in that cañon, where I fancy Nichemus is on watch, and where we'd be helpless if anything happened. Well, get ready and meet me in Montenay's shack. I've got to rout out some food the first thing."

She nodded and turned to obey. Barr watched her lithe, slender figure vanish in the doorway, then started for the other shack, with a vow that if it was humanly possible to pull through he would do it for the sake of this girl.

"What a character she has!" he muttered to himself. "Poor girl, I haven't the nerve to tell her about her father; and it's going to break her all up when we get out."

In order to obviate the chances of pursuit by Montenay, he stopped at Talking Owl's lodge, where he smashed the chief's musket and slashed the gut of his snow-shoes through and through, then went on to the shack. His first attention was devoted to the arsenal.

The flintlock, evidently a relic of older days, he left, together with the shotgun; the others he effectually ruined for further service, while the cartridges he took to the door and scattered by handfuls in the snow.

While he was thus engaged Noreen joined him, her small snow-shoes on her back, and an involuntary cry rose from her as she realized what he was doing.

"It does go against the grain," he admitted ruefully, flinging out a last handful of cartridges and stuffing his pockets with the rest; "but—well, I guess Montenay will be howling mad when he sees his rifles! Serves the brute right, too!"

"But it seems a horrible waste, Barr—especially when you've

been trained all your life to value a cartridge as a possible human life, like I have! Of course, I suppose it's necessary."

"Highly so," said Radison. "We're going to do this thing in thorough fashion, Noreen; and now, if you'll be good enough to get Montenay's sled around to the door I'll prospect for grub."

His search was speedily rewarded by finding most of the tinned goods brought from Fort Tenacity stowed away beneath Montenay's couch. Flour, peas, and other necessities of the white man's trail were also there; and he gave a grunt of satisfaction when Noreen reported that the sled was ready for loading.

"Good! Next job, bring over some whitefish and pemmican from Talking Owl's *starchigan,* and we'll load up."

While she departed for the raised platform where the meat was kept out of reach of dogs or wolverines, Radison started a fire on Montenay's staked-out mud fireplace. After selecting enough provisions for three weeks, he ruthlessly seized an ax and smashed the rest, flinging what was left of flour and peas on the fire.

"There's no chance of Montenay's starving," he reassured Noreen gleefully, "and I want him to remember my visit. Say, aren't we making a dandy wreck out of this old place! Bet a dollar Crazy Bear throws seven kinds of fits!"

Though she smiled at his boyish enthusiasm in the work of destruction, Noreen rebuked him gravely enough.

"It's wrong, Barr; and I'm sorry. Oh, I know that its loss won't cause any starvation, but I can't help feeling it isn't right. Well, I'm a very foolish girl, perhaps; so we'll forget all about it."

"We will not," retorted Barr promptly, smiling at her anxious face. "This stuff was all brought here for your benefit, and I want to show Montenay what I think of his neat little scheme."

It was on his tongue's end to speak of her father's death, but he checked himself abruptly.

"These things are luxuries, not necessities, and our friend of the beard will get a gentle hint that he needn't keep 'em in stock any more. That's not so very bad, is it?"

She repaid his logic with a smile, and they soon had the sled loaded, Noreen's small snow-shoes being tied on behind and a couple of heavy bearskins provided for her comfort, together with an outer capote and hood of beaver.

Satisfied that everything was aboard, from tea-pail to matches, Barr procured Montenay's shoes from the *starchigan* behind the shack, got into a pair of heavy outer moccasins, took down the long dog-whip, and went for the huskies.

Harnessing a team of huskies is an art peculiar to itself, and Radison was forced to come down to sheer Indian whip-brutality before it was accomplished. As she got on the sled Noreen threw a last glance at the shack and laughed.

"I'll be willing to bet anything that when Talking Owl sees this place he won't call you Strong Eyes any more," she laughed gaily. "Only one name will fit you now—Carcajou! It looks exactly as it a wolverine had broken in and worked his will."

Barr grinned as he strapped his rifle to the sled beside her. He had heard many tales of the wondrous destruction that Carcajou, as the wolverine is called in the north, could effect in a short time; indeed, destruction seems second nature to the animal, and the aptness of the name was not lost on him.

"You left enough fire to keep Talking Owl from freezing? All right—we're off! *Mash, mash,* you brutes!"

Handing Noreen the whip, which she knew well how to wield, he strode ahead to break trail and headed for the west. In five minutes the village was lost among the trees behind, and with a thrill of exultation Radison began to put Macklin's teachings into practise; for picking a dog-rail in the woods, with a girl-laden sled behind, is a delicate matter.

Once amid the thicker trees, the oppressive, deathlike stillness of the forest closed down upon them. A faint cloud of frost-powdered snow rose from the dragging heels of the shoes, and the breath of the dogs stood out like smoke, but there was no sound save the sluff of the snow-shoes and the crunch of snow beneath the sled.

The sun was on the horizon, of course, but the whole sky was aflame with fire—bands of rainbow-light and suns that blazed in futile glory.

"Those sundogs mean snow, don't they?" Radison cried back to the girl.

"Perhaps, but not always."

He nodded and swung about again to the trail, and after this no word passed between them for hours. Once Barr was startled by something that looked like a figure flitting through a clump of trees on the left, but he saw nothing more of it, and concluded that he had been mistaken.

Mile after mile reeled behind them as the hours passed, and very slowly the sky banked up, gray, lowering, threatening. Radison pushed the dogs faster, for the gap in the hills was close at hand, and he was determined to reach it before the storm broke.

It had been nearer twenty miles away than ten, but as they neared it he saw that here the abrupt, jagged cliffs ended and became low hills. Farther ahead the rock barrier began again, but the fact that here was an opening spurred the American on.

Closer and closer they drew, and still the storm held off, until there stretched a mile of open ground ahead, with the ending of the cliffs beyond. As they left the trees a little cry broke from Noreen, and Radison looked around to see the country to the north blotted out by a wall of white.

"All right," he called back; "use the whip, and we'll keep going, Noreen!"

The long lash curled and cracked, again and again, but before they had gone a hundred yards the storm was upon them with a howl, snow cloaking them in a white blanket that shut out everything twenty feet away. Radison had fixed his direction, however, and he pushed forward desperately, doggedly fighting his way across the wind and driving cloud of whiteness.

Suddenly a cry of astonishment broke from him, and as he

ran he shielded his face with his mittens, peering ahead. There, a dim gray figure amid the blinding snow, was a man! Barely had he seen it when it vanished from sight, and as he came to the snow-shoe print, already half covered up, he found the heart-shaped track of a Cree shoe!

If Noreen had seen it, she said nothing, and this was no time for talk. Friend or enemy, some man was ahead of them. Radison dared not even go back to the sled for his rifle lest he lose the sense of direction, but kept plunging forward, the whimpering dogs close on his heels. But for that shoe-print Barr would have dismissed the incident as a wild hallucination, for it was inconceivable that a man should pass so close and not see them.

Now he found, however, that there was indeed a man ahead, for his snow-shoes struck into the broken trail, and he kept to it in hope that it would bring them to the shelter of the hills. It was a mad thing to do, but at last he flung all direction to the winds and held the soft trail, feeling for it at each step.

Of a sudden he realized that he was toiling up a steep slope, and though the blast of wind and snow all but tore him from his feet, blind hope thrilled into his heart, and a moment later a dim outline rose ahead. They had reached the hills!

Still he kept the hidden trail, which brought him to clumps of fir and spruce and jack-pine, whistling in the wind. Then the driving snow ceased and became a straight, windless fall; with a single gasp of weary thankfulness Radison saw that he had come into a little valley in the hills, and paused.

"I guess we'll have to ride out the storm," he shouted, bending over the befurred figure on the sled. "Are you hungry?"

"No," and out of the furs the bright face of Noreen smiled up at him. "Just bank the sled on the hillside, and we'll sleep it out."

She held out a ready ax, and Barr knew well enough what to do. Helping her from the sled, he took the blankets and furs, carried them to the slope at one side, and scraped away a large hollow with ax and snow-shoe in the deep drifts. On the up-hill side of this he placed the sled, the dogs huddling around it; then he took the ax and started for the scrub-trees they had passed. A moment more and the snow had closed about him.

Swiftly cutting a heap of fir-branches, he carried them back, clubbed the dogs out of the hollow and spread the fir. Over this he put the bear-skins, wrapped a blanket about Noreen, and placed her next the sled, lying down at her side.

They were instantly banked in by the whining, shivering dogs, and Radison, utterly exhausted by that last desperate spurt for shelter, dropped asleep with the howl of the wind overhead ringing in his ears. He was too weary even to speak of that great man shape in the snow, whose trail had led them to this shelter.

He was roused by a faint cry and deep growls, while heavy bodies trampled him. Sitting up, he found that a foot of snow had covered him, that the sun was streaming over the hills; and that the horde of savage dogs were piled over him and Noreen tearing at the skin coverings of the sled.

"Awus! Awus!" he yelled angrily, seizing the snake-whip and laying about with the loaded butt until the dogs slunk away. He turned to find Noreen flushed, disheveled, but smiling, emerging from her furs.

"Good morning!" she laughed. "I was dreaming about wolves, and thought they were all around me! Did I scream?"

"I believe you said something," smiled Barr. "They didn't get through the lashings, so no harm's done. What a morning it is! I feel like whooping it up—*ki-yi-i-i-i!*"

As he recklessly executed a war-dance and shrilled out the Cree war-cry, Noreen was seized with a fit of laughter that brought him to himself and he sheepishly took up the ax.

"For laughing at me you get to work and feed the dogs," he commanded, "while I start a fire."

"Aha, ne napam," she murmured in mock humility, and Radison started off in blissful ignorance that she had used a Cree formula of wifely obedience, while she looked after him for an instant with merry eyes.

Free! That was the great thought in Radison's mind as he built up a fire and melted snow for the tea. Out of Montenay's hands, on the road to—where? He chuckled and spoke his thought aloud.

"I don't know where we'll end up, but I don't care particularly! Hurray for freedom and the Declaration of Independence! Say, won't Montenay be wild about this time, Noreen? I'd give a dollar to see his face when he gets home! No guns, no cartridges, no dogs, no snow-shoes—oh, he's a great little old king, he is!"

"We aren't out of the woods yet," returned Noreen, her face suddenly grave. "If he can get the Chipewas in from the grounds they'll be on our trail soon enough."

"How? With the snow covering it?"

She nodded. "Of course! They have only to feel down through the new snow to the old crust, and once they strike the trail they'll follow it forever—" she broke off with a little shudder. The words recalled to Radison the figure he had seen the day before.

"I suppose you didn't see any one during that storm yesterday, did you?" he asked carelessly in order not to alarm the girl. "I thought I saw a man, but it might have been a tree in the snow."

"No, I was too busy whipping up the dogs," and a startled look crossed her face as she met Radison's gaze. He nodded reassuringly and turned away to hide the glow that must have swept into his eyes.

"Gad, what a wonder of a girl!" he thought to himself. By some odd brain-twist his mind went back to a certain conversation with Take-a-chance Macklin, and he chuckled. "Just reach out and grip youth again—like getting your second wind! I guess old Mack spoke truth there, right enough. Feel like I'd got a grip on youth and everything else, and I don't give a—by golly! I wonder if she's tied up to any fellow down in Quebec?"

"Don't look so serious, please—and you really aren't supposed to *boil* tea, you know," came the laughing words, and Barr awoke to his duties with a start.

That glorious morning sent them off on the trail with new vigor; but now Radison found that his difficulties had only begun. He cut straight in through the hills that first day, but with the next morning he was in hopeless bewilderment, for all about him lay little hills, too steep for climbing, and the narrow valleys seemed but a tortuous maze of ways that had no direction and no ending.

Twice during the days that followed they traveled for miles on the frozen bed of some little stream only to find that it ended in abrupt precipice, and the way had to be retraced. By dint of lucky guesswork Radison managed to keep their course in a general southerly direction, but the twisting valleys baffled him, and although the two used every precaution of woodcraft, the fear of pursuit lay heavily upon them like an evil shadow.

Many of the hills were bare masses of rock, swept clear of snow, and more than once Radison was forced to unload the sled and carry it across a stretch of bleak rock, for the frail, light craft would have been ripped to pieces had the dogs drawn it. Try as he would he could find no way out of that terrible labyrinth of hills and valleys, for from each crest that he mounted the view was ever the same, with no sight of level barrens to beckon him on.

And yet Radison was not altogether cheerless. For one thing there was no indication of pursuit, and for another, those few days of trail comradeship brought him closer to Noreen Murphy than weeks of other life would have done.

Five days can effect a great deal on the trail, and almost insensibly, while he endeavored to keep the girl's spirits up with stories of his wanderings, he found himself opening to her the gates of his personality, while she opened hers in return.

She told of her early life—of the mother she had never seen—of her days in Quebec at the convent school—of the hard-fisted trader whom she looked forward to seeing again with a joy that shook Radison, for he knew that father and daughter had parted trails forever.

It was on the sixth morning as they were crossing one of the bleak, windswept rock stretches that Noreen halted suddenly and pointed at something to one side near their camp of the night before. Running to it, Radison gazed speechless at a tiny pile of rock fragments, in which had been wedged a wooden cross with one extended arm that pointed to an intersecting valley below. There was no footprint on the rock, and the snow was bare as far as he could see.

"If that's a pointer," he said, rising from his inspection, "it was probably placed there by Montenay—"

"No!" broke in the girl excitedly. "There is fresh snow under the stones!"

Barr stared around, but there was no sign of life among the hills. With a shrug of hopelessness he picked up his load and started forward.

"Whatever it is we'll follow it. I guess Montenay was right when he said we'd never get out of here, Noreen. Come along— we've grub enough for another two weeks."

The valley to which the pointer directed them proved to be fairly open, but Barr was too used to discouragement by this time to feel much confidence. That night, while Noreen prepared supper, he climbed the hill above to cut some wood, carrying his rifle with him as always.

Returning through the tortuous valley he was suddenly startled by the sound of voices, and when he turned a corner and saw the fire ahead, he dropped ax and wood and stripped the casing from his rifle in feverish haste.

For there, calmly talking with Noreen, was a short, powerful figure whose two-horned hood betrayed its identity. The man's back was toward Radison, his cased rifle swung on his arm, and Barr covered him instantly.

"Put up your hands and drop that gun, Jean Nichemus!" he commanded sternly, and strode forward, finger on trigger.

CHAPTER IX

THE CUNNING OF THE BREED

NICHEMUS OBEYED the command to the extent of dropping his rifle—the same which he had taken from Radison weeks before. The grim lines of Barr's face flung his eagle-nose into high relief as he came forward, and Noreen drew a step to one side, her eyes alight with anxiety.

"Well," snapped the American harshly, kicking away the cased rifle, "now you've found us, what are you going to do about it? Been trailing us, I suppose?"

Slowly, very slowly the other smiled and nodded, and Barr felt an indefinable sense of something beyond his ken.

"Four, five days ago," said Nichemus, his soft, liquid voice directed rather at the girl than at Radison, "I see me de smoke. I go for de village, see de king—Gee Cri, he's be de madman! He's cuss an' swear an' say for go fin' dat dam' Carcajou."

Noreen flashed one swift glance at Radison, and he smiled involuntarily. Nichemus grinned.

"So I make for fin' de trail; but de Ghos' Hills, she's be ver' bad. One night de debil he's steal my tea-pail, de nex' night he's take my *usamuk,* so I make me de bear-paw an' come on."

For the first time Radison noticed that Nichemus was wearing rough snow-shoes made from a bent willow wand with skin thongs stretched across—rude, but serviceable affairs that had probably been made in a couple of hours.

"How do you mean—some one stole them?" Nichemus nodded energetic answer to the query.

"I t'ink me de debil he's be in dese hills," was his worried reply. Radison turned to the girl, watching Jean warily.

"He must have just come up?"

"Just before you came," replied Noreen, her face troubled. "He had only said that he meant no harm and asked if I wanted to get out of the hills when you arrived. You won't hurt him, Barr?"

"H-m! That depends on him," said the American slowly. "Noreen, will you please walk down the trail out of earshot? I want to say some things to Jean, and it might not make very nice listening for you."

Noreen's face changed, betraying its hidden strength suddenly, but before she could speak Nichemus broke in quietly with his slow grin.

"I t'ink me you bettair go, Minebegonequay. We make for cuss, mebbe."

Noreen turned and walked down the trail, leaving Radison white with anger—unreasoning anger that she should do it at the breed's request and not at his. When she had turned the corner he flung up his rifle, his brown eyes blazing, but his voice cold.

"Now, Jean Nichemus, you've come to a show-down. You're here uninvited, and I think you're going to stay here. I'd just as soon shoot you as I would a snake, but not before Miss Murphy, so here's your choice: either take oath by all you hold sacred that you'll guide us out of here, or say your prayers. Hurry up. I've no time to waste on you!"

For just an instant the deadly determination in his voice blanched the brown cheek of Nichemus; then the other drew himself up with inborn dignity, dark eyes flashing.

"*M'sieu*, you be de beeg fool. You go to de debil!"

His cold rage heightened by the defiance, Radison pressed the trigger. But before the hammer fell something checked him—a thin, eery wail that seemed to come from the very sky above, and that froze him into awed immobility, so fine, yet faint and piercing was that voice.

"Nichemus! Nichemus! Have you forgotten me?"

Radison was astounded at the sudden change in the other. For an instant the breed's gaze flew to the hills and sky, then his face became a sickly white, he staggered back and clapped his hands over his eyes with a shuddering groan.

"*Achak!* A ghost!"

Weird as the cry had been, Radison had small faith in ghosts, and raised his voice.

"Who's there, Noreen?"

The girl's voice came from behind him, and there was only relief on her face when she appeared.

"What is it, Barr—why, Jean! What's the matter?"

"De Ghos' Hills!" moaned Nichemus, removing his hands and staring around with ghastly features. "You hear heem—de *bon* Père Sulvent?"

The evident amazement of the girl woke Barr from his momentary stupor.

"Didn't you hear anything, Noreen?" His voice was hoarse despite his self-control.

"Why, I thought I heard a wolf howl, but that was all! What has happened?"

"I—nothing," returned Radison slowly. "We must have been mistaken."

His eyes went to Nichemus, and for a long moment the two men stared at each other, their antagonism forgotten. Before Barr had rallied himself the breed flung out both hands in a helpless gesture.

"I will make for be de guide, *m'sieu!* See, on *le bon Dieu* I swear!"

"Very well," returned Radison, now master of himself. He knew that Nichemus would never break that oath, for the breed was fumbling a crucifix plucked from his breast. "Will you see about making tea for all of us, Noreen? I want to take a little walk, and Jean has consented to guide us out of the hills."

"Hurrah!" cried Noreen delightedly. "Come along, Jean, you get that pemmican out!"

Radison walked down the little winding valley in blank bewilderment, staring at the rocky walls above. The thing was incredible. Nichemus had recognized the voice as that of Père Sulvent, the priest who had vanished six months before, and who owed his death to Montenay, supposedly.

Yet, Père Sulvent was dead! "Sulvent is as dead as Murphy, rest his soul!" He recalled Montenay's words, and glanced around the bleak valley walls with a shiver. Had Noreen heard the voice Radison would have thought nothing of it, for he took small stock in the supernatural; but the girl's words, and the loneliness of the place had combined to shatter his confidence.

"Good Lord, but I *know* I heard it!" he muttered as he searched the naked rock around. "And Jean heard it too, for he went all to pieces. If it was any friend, why the devil should he stick up there and yell?"

Suddenly he remembered the dim shape in the storm, the pointer he and Noreen had seen only that morning in its heap of stones. Could it be possible that some unknown friend was helping them? No, he decided promptly, for that friend would have no reason to conceal himself; yet—-

"Confound it!" he cried angrily as he swung about and started back to camp. "That ghost business won't go down with me! There's a man around here somewhere, and by Godfrey he can't put anything over on me! This is no time for monkey-work, and if there are any more tricks played I'll shoot first and explain afterward, that's all."

Feeling thoroughly angered at his own helplessness, Barr walked into camp and silently fell to work feeding the dogs. Nichemus had by no means gotten over his fright, and with grim enjoyment Radison, when the meal was done, lit his pipe and turned the talk on Père Sulvent.

"Funny how he disappeared, wasn't it? Ever hear anything about it, Jean?"

Nichemus puffed silently for a moment, his narrowed eyes roving about.

"Non, m'sieu, Dey say he wen' out for fin' de king; but he's nevair come back."

"He did?" broke in Noreen, leaning forward with sudden interest. "Where did you hear that, Jean?"

"De king, she's say so one day," Nichemus was plainly uneasy, and like all breeds, the more uneasy he got the less intelligible he grew. "She's been de ver' queer t'ing—" with which he went off on an interminable story which was seemingly designed to stave off further questioning, but which only served to irritate Radison.

"Oh, cut that out!" he interrupted impatiently. "Did Montenay kill him?"

Nichemus looked at him, and in the breed's face he read an almost childish bewilderment and horror. The man plainly knew nothing, and dreaded his own fears.

"M'sieu, I don't know! If I t'ink so I make for keel de king—by Goss, *oui!"*

"Don't talk about it!" exclaimed Noreen with a shudder, her face very drawn and tired. "We all loved him, Barr, and—and I think I'll get some sleep."

Radison nodded and conducted her to the brush wind-break which Nichemus had thrown up, for now he and the breed would lie together with the dogs. It never entered his head to suspect treachery, for Jean had sworn the oath inviolate that no breed would break even under torture. As he rolled up in his blanket his last remembrance was of Nichemus brooding over the fire and slowly mixing killikinick with his tobacco, while the huskies lay about in their simulation of sleep.

With the morning Nichemus tacitly assumed command of the dogs, and by midday Radison had totally lost every sense of direction. Jean led them back and forth, over frozen streams, through rocky defiles, and as a dull gray mantle of cloud hid the sky and sun from view, Radison finally abandoned himself to the inevitable, and merely plodded along behind the sled, rifle over his shoulder.

His thoughts wandered far away to the comrades who had lost him. Where was Macklin; where was Uchichak, now? That they had given him up was not to be dreamed of, and hope revived in him at thought of meeting them again and gripping good old Take-a-chance by the hand.

During three days they wound among the Ghost Hills, and by this time the American hated the very sight of the narrow defiles and bleak pinnacles of rock, where not a bird or animal was to be found, and where even the golden snow-buttercups were missing. Jean pushed them at a stiff pace, which tested Barr's new strength to the utmost, but he was too anxious to be away from the place to complain.

In those three days he noted a strange manner in Nichemus. The breed was very silent, brooded over the fire at night, watched the peaks by day, clubbed one of the dogs unmercifully when they overran his shoes and flung him in the snow, and eyed Radison with strange looks that boded a gathering storm.

There was storm in the sky, also, for all during those three days the gray clouds never lifted and no gleam of sunshine brightened the gloom of the hills. Radison felt that he was losing his grip; the slightest thing seemed to irritate him strangely, and the desolation around him seemed to be driving him mad.

With the fourth morning all changed. Returning sullenly with a load of wood, Barr found Nichemus talking earnestly with Noreen, and the girl turned to him with a smile.

"Give me your rifle, Barr, will you?"

He watched her strap the weapon to the sled, but said nothing. During breakfast Nichemus sat apart repairing his rude snow-shoes, and for the first time he seemed in a cheerful mood, for his rich voice rang out in an old song of the south, and he grinned cheerfully between the lines.

"Fille du roi,
Donne moi, va, ton cœur,
Et ri, et ran,

> Rampe-ta-plan,
> Donne moi, va, ton cœur!"

While he was harnessing the dogs Noreen beckoned Radison aside, her cheeks tinged with red.

"A surprise for you, Barr! Nichemus told me that by night we'll be out of the hills!"

"Thank the Lord!" ejaculated Radison wearily, biting his lips as he spoke. "There's something—I don't know—oh, I have a feeling that everything's gone to pieces, Noreen! It's these silent, dead, lonesome hills that are enough to tear the soul out of a fellow!"

"I know," she nodded. "But listen, Barr—that's not all. Jean is terribly worried about something, and I want you to promise me one thing, though I don't quite understand it myself. Promise me that whatever you see or hear you'll let Jean explain."

"Explain? Explain what?" repeated Radison, on the alert instantly. "Is something wrong?"

"I'm not sure myself," answered the girl anxiously; "but he's afraid of your temper, for some reason, and I think he really means well."

"All right," laughed Barr. "I'll promise not to lay a finger on him until he talks his heart out, Noreen. So that's why you wanted the gun, eh?"

She smiled, and they returned to the waiting team, Radison throwing one curious glance at Nichemus. He had long since given up puzzling over the mysteries that presented themselves, and merely slapped along behind the sled in dour silence, too soul-weary even to seek consolation from his pipe.

Shortly after four in the afternoon he saw Jean suddenly quicken the pace, uncasing his rifle; staring around, Barr felt a thrill as he saw a great, open stretch of snow and trees through the mouth of the defile ahead. Five minutes later he was staring with incredulous eyes at the scene before him.

For there, beyond the woods and barrens below the great cliff on which they stood, was the Chipewa village! For an instant Radison looked, then his hand went to his knife and there was murder in the gaunt, bloodless face as he kicked free of his shoes and turned on Nichemus, remembering his promise.

"You dog!" he said in a cold rage, his bloodshot eyes gleaming. He put out a hand and brushed Noreen aside. "Now speak, for, by the living God, you die when you get through!"

Nichemus quietly put down his rifle and came back to the sled, looking only at the girl, and there was that in his eyes which sent her hand to the arm of Radison.

"Minebegonequay," he said softly, utterly disregarding the American, "I promise' to make for guide you out of de Ghos' Hills, *non?* So I keep me dat promise! Lissen, girl! For de long year I been come on de w'ite *tabac* pos', an' each day *le bon Dieu* she's say to me, 'Jean, dere's be *une ange,* an angel from de Paradise, on de pos'! You's be de good trappair, de good man, mebbe I make for give you dis *ange, oui!'*"

For a moment the breed paused, and when he went on his liquid voice had become hoarse but vibrant with earnestness.

"*M'sieu,* all de long year Minebegonequay she's be de one star up in de sky for me, she's make me de good man, she's make me hear de good *père*—ah, she's be all de worl', *m'sieu!* I t'ink me, some day I fin' de black-fox, I keel de king for make her happy, but always de king make me 'fraid. Den he go for steal de star, an' always I watch, I wait for keel him w'en de Silen' Ones forget, mebbe.

"I want for say dis, Minebegonequay. I be de good trappair; I nevair drink de w'iskey, I got me one, two shack wit' plenty skin; I go to de mass ever' year, an' I love you, Minebegonequay! Make for marry me, we go—"

"That's enough," Radison's voice was almost a whisper, but it seemed to bite through the vibrant tones of Nichemus as steel bites flesh. "God help you, Jean Nichemus! Finish, and quickly!" He quietly replaced the knife in its sheath and loosened his mittens.

The breed flashed him a single look of scorn.

"If you keel, how you get out, huh? Minebegonequay, say you's make for marry me, we go ver' quick! Oh, *ma belle*, I's be ver' good to you all de time!" His voice broke.

White and trembling, Noreen tried to speak but could not, and again Radison interrupted.

"If she marries you, then you will take us out of here, eh? And if not—what?"

"If not"—and the restrained passion of the man burst all bounds in its wild frenzy—"if not, den, by Goss, I make for keel de king an' you an' her an'—ah, *non, non, non!* Not dat! I don' know—I t'ink me I be de crazy man! Say *oui*, den we go on de pos' an' make for—"

"You're done!" snapped Radison, his hands trembling and the veins standing out on his brow with repressed fury. Noreen uttered one stifled cry of terror and turned, stumbling over the snow in wild fear as the American, with a red mist before his eyes, locked his fingers in the throat of Nichemus and bore him down in the midst of the snarling dogs.

CHAPTER X

THE FLAT-SHOE TRACK

FLICKERING DREAM-FANCIES came and fled in the darkness. Barr knew he was on the sled, and tied down, for he could feel the ropes, and the ghosts had done it all—ghosts of the hills! No, there were no ghosts, but the horrible face of Nichemus, slowly throttling under him, the dogs snapping madly, the shriek of Noreen in his ears!—something terrible that fell on him and wrenched him away and flung him out into space and down, down—

Radison opened his eyes and stared into the blackness, cold sweat on his face and body. He tried to move, and found himself bound hand and foot. What had happened? Had that terrible wandering through the hills been a mad dream? A wrenching pain in his arms was answer to the contrary, and he came to himself with a groan.

He had failed, then! He remembered a wild battle in the snow-spume—dogs and men together—and then oblivion. As he lay there in the darkness the sound of voices slowly pierced through returning consciousness, and with a terrible sense of helplessness he recognized the deep tones of Montenay. A single sob of utter despair burst upon him, then he lay quiet, listening.

"Jean, ye can thank King Montenay for savin' your worthless hide! He had ye gone when I jumped him—God! what a man to fight! Shut up, ye fool, and take another drink! When I'm talkin' you keep your trap shut, unless you want to lay along o' Père Sulvent and Murphy! What's that—growl at me, will ye? You scum o' purgatory; for two cents I'd break your back! Oh, I heard it all—the Chipewas were watchin' you! Thought ye'd take my wife, hey?"

"*Non, m'sieu!* She care not for you," came a wild, incoherent protestation from Nichemus, whose voice sounded wheezy and hoarse. "De ghos' of Père Sulvent—"

"Sulvent's ghost! Ho, ho!" Montenay laughed drunkenly. "Down among the dead men—let—him—*lie!* I'll lay his ghost where he lies, under fifty foot o' snow, with a bullet in his brain! Why, the sneak thought he'd spy on King Montenay, he did! What's that? Say it again or I'll tear it out of ye, man!"

"I say you be de debil," shrilled Nichemus wildly. "You make for keel *le bon père,* eh? Den hees ghos', he come for—for—ah-r-r-r—"

Silence. Radison felt the sweat start on his brow as the hoarse, throaty cry died away, for now he knew everything. It was Montenay who had interfered, and the giant was strangling Nichemus in the next room.

"Now, you lie there an' listen," the deep voice rumbled forth in terrible softness as a low moan of pain was wrung from the other. "Do you know what I'll do with you, Jean? I'll take you to the place of the Silent Ones to-night. You remember how Pierre Radisson looked across the table at you? I'll take you there and tie you down—tie you with your hand in his, and I'll put the two painted chiefs beside you and leave you in the darkness, with the water falling on your hand, drip—drip—drip—"

"*Ah-h-h!*"

One long-drawn scream of agony broke forth, followed again by that soft, tense rumble.

"No? Then swear on this crucifix that you'll obey me in all things, Jean! Ye're a good man, in your way—"

Mercifully Barr fainted!

When consciousness came again it was with a restful feeling, and he lay with closed eyes, while a soft hand wandered over his brow, bringing him a sense of delicious peace. Then he barely repressed a quick shudder as he heard Montenay's voice again; but this time it was sober, with all its old richness and timbre.

"An' how is he, Noreen?"

"No change as yet. Thank you for sending Jean away, Montenay."

"I'd do anything to please ye, Noreen! Aye, he's gone to gather the warriors for the wedding. Poor Radisson, I'd cut off my right hand to win him over! Ye'll mind your promise, girl? He's done more damage in his madness than a dozen other men, and I love him for it; but if he cuts loose again the Chipewas will finish him—and the Lord preserve him from them!"

"I'll remember," came the low voice of Noreen, and a door slammed. A moment later Barr felt a weight on his breast, and a little sob sounded. "Oh, Strong Eyes, I need you—I need you!"

Opening his eyes, Barr found himself alone with Noreen, who knelt at his side. He put out a hand and laid it on her head, and she looked up, startled at the touch.

"Put your head down again, Noreen dear," he said very softly, and drew the loose mass of golden hair to him until her face was crushed against his heart. For a long time they remained thus, speaking no word, and Barr knew that at last he had entered into the Land of Heart's Desire.

"Tell me, dear," he said at last, "where am I, and what has happened?"

Once more the violet eyes met his, and now there was something in them that he had never seen in woman's eyes since the day he knelt to bid his mother farewell—a tenderness that was too great for words.

"It was four days ago, Barr—dear. Montenay and a dozen Chipewas were waiting for us, and they tore you and Jean apart. Montenay hurt your arms, but not badly."

"But—but tell me what you promised him!"

The fear in Barr's soul crept into his face, and Noreen smiled softly down, understanding.

"I promised not to try to escape if he would unbind you and take care of you, dear. What a terrible man he is! Sometimes he's wonderfully gentle and kind—he sent Jean away because I was afraid to have him here. Now, remember, I promised that you would be good if he let you loose, because the Chipewas are horribly uneasy at the thought of your being free. You've made quite an impression, Strong Eyes!"

"I thought you'd named me Carcajou?" he smiled up at her, relief surging in him.

"I—I like Strong Eyes better," she returned softly, and this time her head did not fall on his shoulder by a matter of several inches.

Inside of two days Barr discovered a good many things. He found that he was in good shape except for his wrenched shoulders, and that Montenay was conciliatory; that violet eyes could attain the most unfathomable depths of tenderness, and that he was quite satisfied to lie still by the hour while certain soft hands were his to hold.

Montenay observed nothing of all this. The giant was courting Noreen in his own fashion, which consisted largely in sending gifts. He seemed to be wrapped in an assured self-complacency which dreamed of no rival and which counted the game already won. Radison managed to hide his secret anxiety from Noreen, but he knew that they were in desperate case, and prayed hourly for some sign of Tom Macklin, which came not.

On the third day Barr was moved to his former wigwam, and the existence in the village went on as it had before the escape, for Noreen had promised to remain and Radison could not prevail on her to withdraw the promise.

"No, dear, it's better not. We could never escape from here now, with the hunters home again, and I want to keep you safe while I can. I'll never marry him—oh, it's too horrible to talk about!"

"Oh, well, I'll be good," sighed Barr with a half-smile. "Sooner or later things will come to a head, Noreen. Then it'll be either me or Montenay—and I have a notion that it'll be Montenay who'll lose. Anyway, I've won the greatest game of all, Noreen dear!"

Which was some comfort, as Radison admitted to himself.

Now, the American fully intended to "be good," as Noreen phrased it, both for his own sake and for hers. Fighting was not a thing he liked or longed for, but he accepted the need when it arose, just as he accepted everything else, in a grim, uncompromising spirit.

He had long since learned the great fact that the best man is the man who hits first and hits hardest, and when he had to use his fists he practised that simple philosophy with his whole soul. Moreover, his temper had never been a meek one, and the course of events leading up to his final outbreak was not calculated to soothe his spirit.

The first incident came while he stood in the doorway of his lodge and watched the Chipewas preparing the meat they had brought in. Talking Owl nodded to him with a grin, but Yellow Wolf flung out a snarling phrase in his own tongue which brought a laugh to the other dark faces, and Radison felt the flush that swept to his face.

He restrained himself, however, and at a hasty word from Talking Owl the other fell silent, while Barr strode past without a word. During that brief instant he had seen the hands creeping up to belt-knives, and realized his danger.

"This powder-mine will go up with a bang yet," he muttered angrily, and the angrier he grew the more menacing his face became. "But I've got to save Noreen from that brute, and I'm darned if I know how to do it!"

He had been carefully stripped of weapons, even his knife being taken, for the Indians held his prowess in obvious respect. He found that at night his lodge was unguarded, but the caribou-skin door flap was lashed in place from the outside, which effectually prevented egress, for the mud-banked lodge-poles were too solidly placed to be broken through. During the day, however, no hindrance was offered to his wandering at will, so he and Noreen resumed their walks along the ridges under the great cliffs above the village.

More than once he remembered how Montenay had vanished there in that black cañon which lay dark and ominous in the brightest day, with the high cliffs folding it in; but although he made two attempts to enter the cleft that led down into the hills and the earth-bowels, each time a Chipewa had appeared and silently motioned him back.

Nor was this a thing to calm him overmuch, for he had all the white man's resentment at receiving orders from one of another race.

They had now been back in the village for a week, but Barr had lost all track of time, and one day was as another to him. None the less, slowly but surely the little trivial incidents were building up to a climax—a muttered word from Yellow Wolf, a half-bared knife, and one morning he found a little heap of caribou-offal at his door.

Then he realized his danger, for the Chipewas were deliberately tempting him to break out and give them excuse to knife him. Radison strode over to Montenay's shack and found the giant working on a broken rifle-stock.

"Was this placed at my door by your orders?" demanded Barr, his nostrils quivering slightly. Montenay gave one look, then dashed past him, and with a roar collected the Chipewas.

During the next ten minutes Radison longed to understand Chipewa. The giant lashed the dozen braves with his tongue until they shrank back before him, all save one man whose hand went to his knife, and him Montenay stretched senseless with a blow.

Finally Talking Owl made a half-hearted response, and Montenay returned to pull Radison inside the shack.

"Come in, man. Why have ye not been to see me before—do you hate me so?"

"No," rejoined Barr coldly. "I can even imagine that under other circumstances you would be an extremely likable chap, Montenay—but you're a devil when the drink is in you, no less!"

"Aye, it's true," and the giant drooped his head until the great beard merged with the bearskin capote he had flung on. He stared moodily at the American, and once more Barr felt that odd wistfulness in his manner.

"It's true, Radisson—and I know it. If it wasn't for the liquor, man, I'd be an officer and a gentleman, save the mark! But what's done is done. You're a bit of a devil at times yourself, friend.

"Oh, Radisson, if ye but stood with me and not against me! There are riches for the having—skins such as London and Paris never saw the like of—and there's empire for the taking, no less! A hundred Chipewas over the empty places, a bit o' headwork to keep the Crees quiet, and in a year we could drift a thousand Chipewas an' Jibways up from the south, with never a word to the Dominion until all was done.

"I've been working for it, and it's feasible, man! You heard me talk to those warriors? I have 'em cowed till they'd lick my boots—aye, an' I've made 'em do it! If I but had ye with me,

Barr Radisson, you and I an' Pierre, we'd sweep all the north clean!"

"No chance," and Radison took refuge in his pipe. "As for wealth, I have enough. I don't want power, and I wouldn't live in this God-forsaken country for love or money. It's all right for you, if you like it—you're a caveman, anyway; I'm not. I like to enjoy myself with other people and be a straightaway, ordinary human being. There's one thing that you could do, though. I'd give a good deal to know all about your silent ones and who Pierre Radisson is, and all that."

"Who Radisson is? Why, himself!" The other leaned forward earnestly. "Radisson, it's God's truth that I'm afraid of you. When I tell you that Pierre Radisson is within a mile of here, that you can go and look him in the eye and take his hind, that with him you can meet two chiefs who once led the Mohawks in their raids on Quebec—you have the sense to know that there's either a kink in my yarn or a kink in my brain.

"These Chipewas and breeds haven't the sense. They go and meet the three, and they come away with the marrow frozen in 'em. My system is to keep it frozen, and I manage it pretty well. But if you threw the light o' common sense into 'em, I'd be gone. Give me your friendship, Radisson, for I'd barter my very soul to have it! You're a man."

"One condition," Barr met the flaming eyes coolly. "Take Noreen home!"

"No! I fought God Himself to get her, and I'd murder another priest to keep her."

"Then we can't talk business. Sorry." With which laconic conclusion Barr knocked out his pipe and left the giant's shack, while behind sat Montenay, with head on breast, staring gloomily after the one man whose friendship he craved and could not win.

"Thank Heaven he was sober this morning!" reflected Barr, returning to his lodge. A glance showed him Yellow Wolf leaving toward the south, musket over his shoulder, doubtless to hunt or take up some of his traps, for the braves got a good deal of fur from the stream that wandered through the trees, past the village.

"It'd take a regiment to handle Montenay drunk! Poor devil, he must have liked me from the first, when I knocked him down. Confound my temper! It's sure got me into one nice mess here!"

Two hours later he had forgotten his misgivings as he walked at Noreen's side under the high cliffs where the rock-ledges were bare of snow, and told of his conversation with Montenay. Before he finished Noreen stopped suddenly and caught at his hand.

"Look there, Barr!" she said in a strange tone, pointing down.

In a little patch of snow in a rock-hollow he saw a single clear-cut imprint, and looked back to her face in surprise, for there was nothing unusual in such a track, to his eyes. She was staring down, her cheeks flushed and excitement in her face.

"Well, isn't it just like my own?"

Smiling, Barr pressed his foot on the crust and left a second print. A little cry broke from the girl.

"I knew it! Oh, you blind boy—look, they're both what are called flat-shoes, with a seam on each side of the sole! None of the Chipewas made that print, for they wear single-piece moccasins!"

"By thunder, you're right! And I never made that other print, for we haven't been along here since we got back. Take-a-chance Macklin's here, Noreen! We both got new moccasins from a Saulteaux squaw down at Doobaunt—it's Macklin, or I'm a duffer!"

For a moment they stared into each other's eyes, and Barr restrained a wild impulse to fling his arms about her with a yell. Then he turned, his keen gaze sweeping the deserted barrens and the lonely crags that stretched south and west. No sign of life could be seen, no tiny spiral of smoke tainted the sky, and he was just turning back when, far to the south, near the opening in the cliffs, he caught a tiny flash of red against the black rock.

"A rifle, Noreen." He took her arm and gently turned her toward the village. "Come, we'd better go back, dear. There's nothing to do but to wait—thank God, Macklin has arrived in time!"

CHAPTER XI

THE BREAKING POINT

"**M**ONTENAY WENT off yesterday afternoon," said Barr. It the morning after they had found that flat-shoe track beneath the cliffs. Nothing had happened, no message had come to them from Macklin, and the heavy weight of despondency had settled blackly upon Radison, bringing with it all the devils of moodiness in its train. "I suppose he'll come home drunk. Wish I had a gun!"

"I'm glad you haven't," laughed Noreen, bravely hiding the anxiety in her face. "Do try to be a good boy, Barr!"

"But when I think of you—" He groaned and stopped abruptly.

Montenay was coming toward them from the cliffs, and somewhat to his surprise Barr saw that the giant was sober, and carried a skin packet. Pausing a hundred feet away, he beckoned to Radison and turned to his own shack.

"Suppose I'll have to humor the beast," growled Radison.

"Wipe that brooding-eagle look off your face," and Noreen laughed, an anxious note in her voice. "Please, dear!"

"All right—I'll beard the bear in his den and just grin at him," returned the American, with an attempt at gaiety which he was very far from feeling.

As he walked into Montenay's shack he saw the sight he least expected. The giant had flung off his skins, and the wild tangle of black hair fell about a face that was ghastly pale; the great hands that gripped the skin-packet were trembling as with the ague, and with a gesture toward a seat Montenay sank weakly back on his couch.

"Radisson," he said thickly, "an hour ago I was drunk, raving drunk. Now I'm as sober as you are—and I *heard* it, man! If I'd just seen the thing it wouldn't matter, but I saw it and I heard it—and it pretty near ripped the living innards out o' me!"

He wiped the sweat from his brow, although the shack was fireless and bitterly cold. Radison waited. Evidently something had happened out of the ordinary, for Montenay had completely gone to pieces, but the next words gave him the clue.

"Nichemus told the truth, Radisson, and I thought he lied. Tell me, did ye really hear the voice o' Père Sulvent up there in the hills?"

A thrill ran through Radison. Had Montenay also heard that eery ghost-voice—was this the secret of the pallid brow and shaking hands? Without more ado he told of the happening in the hills, and with grim delight elaborated upon it until Montenay put out a hand.

"Enough, man! Do ye believe in ghosts?"

"Of course," Barr lied cheerfully. "Why not? Why shouldn't a ghost return to haunt a murderer? I knew a man out in the Philippines who had shot a monk, and every night the ghost would come back and howl until the fellow hung himself finally."

Perhaps Montenay perceived his intent, for the bearded face went forward suspiciously and the undershot jaw shoved out.

"Child's tales, man! No ghost can scare Macferris Montenay—for ghosts don't talk! Well—let be. That's not what I wanted to see ye for. A week from to-day I got a little job for ye."

"Yes?"

"Yes—marryin' me an' Noreen."

Barr stared for a moment, but Montenay was evidently in

deadly earnest, and spoke in a matter-of-fact way, tapping the skin-packet.

"Ye see, we got a smoke to-day sayin' that Nichemus and some of the Chipewas would be in to-morrow—travelin' is slow with the squaws, ye know. Well, they'll all be here inside of a week, and it ain't good to keep 'em off the fur grounds too long, so we'll say a week from to-day."

"But, you crazy fool," broke out Radison angrily, "you know I've no right to marry you! It wouldn't be legal—it would be a damned outrage—"

"Tut, tut! I'll give ye the right, man! Don't worry—the prophecy won't come true unless I let it, but you're pretty safe now." Radison saw that with the disappearance of the shock which Montenay must have suffered, the effect of the liquor was coming back on the man.

"I'll give ye the right—take ye to Radisson himself. This is his country, an' I stole it, but ye needn't think ye can take it from me, even if ye do bear his name! What I have I keep, mind that. Here, look at this—Radisson sent it to ye, to use for the wedding."

Barr took the skin packet that Montenay held out, and unwrapped the soft windings of buckskin, disclosing an ancient black-leather Bible. The book seemed in no way remarkable until Barr opened it, and his eyes met the inscription on the fly-leaf, finely written in faded brown ink:

> To My Beloved Husband
> Peter E. Radisson
> London, 1706

And in one corner, in a vigorous, graceful hand, were the words "Sieur Pierre Esprit Radisson, *son livre*."

For a moment Radison forgot the drink-crazed man before him. Could it be possible, by any freak of chance, that this Pierre Radisson was his own ancestor? Barr cared little enough for genealogy, but it was a thrilling thought that this Bible had been owned by one of the greatest Americans of old time, whose name he bore. He was recalled to himself by a maudlin chuckle from Montenay.

"Interests ye, eh? Pierre sent his love with it—hoped ye'd read it o' nights—he, he!" And the giant pulled out a flask, drained it in two gulps, and flung it into the corner.

"Where did you get it, Montenay?" queried Barr. Here was proof positive that the other was not mad, and now for the first time the American began to take a keen interest in the Silent Ones.

"Where? I took it, ye fool!" The giant rose to his feet and clumsily set about building a fire, talking the while. "Right o' conquest—man's got to grab on to what he wants in this world, same as in everything. Want a girl, grab her. Want a book, grab it. Want a throne, grab it—and don't let up for God, man, or devil, though hell's a popping under your feet!

"That's life, and that's the way to beat the game, boy. Don't cut a man's throat, but slam him in the jaw fair an' square. I give Sulvent his warnin', then I put a bullet into him—the cursed fool!"

"Very pretty philosophy, that," said Barr disgustedly. "You're a mere brute of a caveman, Macferris Montenay—and a poor specimen at that. As for marrying you, I'll see you in Gehenna first. Don't try any of your cursed sacrilege around me, or I'll put Père Sulvent's ghost on your heels for good, you hound!"

The words seemed to bring Montenay sober again. He straightened up from the tiny blaze, and Barr saw that his face had blanched once more, while there was a flash of raw fear in his eyes. He silently walked over and took the Bible, which Radison had wrapped up in its skin, and laid it on his couch. When he spoke his voice was unsteady.

"Be careful, man! I've taken that from you for which I'd break another's back, for I like ye. Don't tempt me over the line, Barr Radisson! Ye'll do what I tell ye, and ye'll do it as I tell ye to, mind that."

"All right, friend Montenay. You've had your say—now listen. If you put this ungodly plan of yours' through, I swear on that book that I'll wipe you out of existence like the dog you are!

"I'll go back to the States, I'll bring a thousand men up here if necessary, I'll sweep every corner of the Ghost Hills and the country beyond—but I'll take you and I'll hang you by the neck and flog death into you, so help me God!

"You—telling me to be careful! Why, you've all but tempted *me* over the line, and if I reach the breaking point one of us quits for good. That's *my* say, Montenay, and it goes. Now I'll make no more trouble if I can help it, but if you ruin that girl's life you'll die the death of an Indian dog—or worse."

Barr leaned back, trembling with the intensity of his passion. The words had seemed to bite deep into Montenay's half-crazed brain, and the quiet, deadly ferocity of Barr drove him slowly back like a physical force, his long jaw hanging and his eyes staring.

Then an ugly gleam crossed his face land his beard stuck forward as his jaw settled into place, but he waited for one long moment before speaking, the fists slowly opening and clenching at his sides.

Every trace of drink had left him suddenly, and Radison sensed that something was amiss—that something in his words or his voice or his eyes had loosened the brute in Montenay. He spoke at last, very slowly and softly, as Barr had heard him speak while strangling Jean Nichemus.

"There's one thing that's more than furs, more than Pierre Radisson, more than the Silent Ones and all the kingdom of the north country. I'm afraid I have been a fool, Barr Radisson.

"I thought you wanted the other things, and I played with you. I thought you wanted the empire I had dreamed and had begun to carve out, but now I think you want the one thing above all these—the one thing I'd sell soul and body for—the one thing I'd fight all the angels of heaven and devils of hell to keep—and that's Noreen."

Barr rose to his feet, for with the certainty that the breaking point had come, swift recklessness settled on him.

"Yes, Montenay, you've been a fool. You've lost the whole game for you can never win that woman's love. You've lost the greatest prize of all—and I've won!"

The other still stared, seeming not to hear him, and the eyes of the two men met and gripped—each pair unyielding, indomitable, filled with steady hate. Again that soft, terribly menacing voice sounded.

"The price o' drink, the price o' drink! If I'd kept clean of the liquor I would have known this before, but it's not too late yet. You're a man, Barr Radisson—and I could tear the heart out of you with my hands for this work of yours!

"But I won't. No, I'll do better than that. Radisson said you'd come, but he didn't know that Macferris Montenay would get here first. That prophecy goes into the discard, my lad!

"I think it'd be fine to take you to Pierre on the weddin' day and leave you sitting face to face, hand to hand together! Aye, that would be a proper good joke!"

The American held his eyes on those of Montenay, silent. He knew that at any instant the mood of the giant might change, that Montenay might come forward with a rush, and he almost unconsciously picked out the angle of jaw where his fist would land.

This quiet tension was infinitely more terrific than open battle; but it had come so unexpectedly to both men, the physical had yielded so swiftly to the mental conflict, that each strove to break that struggle of wills, knowing that once the eye-grip went the hand-grip would inevitably follow.

In the tense silence Radison felt acutely sensitive to outside noises. He heard the huskies start a yapping, snarling fight, and heard Talking Owl quiet them with voice and whip. He wondered dully that blind rage had not swept over him, but still his brown eyes held the black ones and never wavered.

A wandering whisky-jack pecked at the window, his chatter

and wing-rustle sounding loud in the frosty stillness, until a spattering crackel of Montenay's fire sent him off into air again.

Then, with startling abruptness, the scene changed. Montenay passed a hand over his eyes and slumped back against the log wall. Barr's tense muscles relaxed, and with startled surprise he saw the giant slowly heave himself up and turn to the door without a word.

A glimpse of the high-boned face, pallid beneath its beard, and Montenay was gone.

The reaction was too much for Barr, and he leaned against the logs, trembling, wondering what the meaning of this action could be. He was not long left in doubt. The door suddenly creaked again, there came a crunch of snow, and into the room stalked Nichemus, whom Radison supposed far away. As the American drew himself together, Talking Owl and two or three more Chipewas crowded in behind the breed.

Radison glanced about for a weapon, but he stood in an empty corner of the shack. He knew full well the futility of trying to overawe such men as these silent, grim sons of the North with any other than the might of fist, and Nichemus walked confidently forward, hand on knife. Radison suddenly launched himself without a second's warning, and his fist struck Jean full on the point of his stocky jaw.

Lifted clean off his feet by that terrific blow, Nichemus whirled back, reeled into Talking Owl, struck out spasmodically with his knife and went down in a huddled heap. The warrior behind Talking Owl uttered a choking cry and fell, for Jean's blind stab had gone through wool capote an shirt and heart, and the two men were locked together.

The American sprang back against the wall, his eyes glittering from his gaunt, terrible face, but he had a brief respite, for, as their comrades went down, the Chipewas had crowded back in horrified amazement.

Talking Owl staggered up and his knife flashed out in silence; without a glance at his men he took a step forward, and Radison

leaped aside just as the spinning steel thudded and quivered in
the logs under his arm. With the same movement he struck
out, and the chief reeled back among his men.

Radison, carried away by the lust of fight, plunged forward
before another knife could be thrown. He struck Talking Owl
again, and smashed his left into another dark face; then, as a
knife ripped through his capote from behind, he whirled before
the steel reached the flesh and flung up his knee. Caught full
in the stomach, the Chipewa who had stolen around him went
back with a gasp and rolled to the floor.

There was no need for more. Terrified at this demon who
killed with his fists and knees, the other two men fled through
the door. Radison was across the floor in a bound, slammed the
heavy door, and put his foot against it in lieu of a bar. Then he
turned to look at the room.

Nichemus lay motionless, and over his dirty white capote
ran a little stream of red from the man who lay across him.
Talking Owl was huddled half over the couch, senseless; and
the Chipewa caught by the deadly knee-punch was gasping
and groaning for air on the floor. Radison smiled grimly, then
whirled at the crunch of snow from without.

"Radisson! Come out or I'll fire the place over you!"

Stooping, the American picked up a naked knife from the
floor and flung the door wide. Radison knew that he had gone
too far now, that not even Montenay could save him from the
Chipewas, and he determined that he would finish with the
giant before he was shot down.

To his amazement, Montenay faced him with empty hands,
and Barr stood motionless, unable to strike, a strange weakness
falling on him.

"I was not minded to have ye killed," said the other dispas-
sionately, "or I'd ha' done it myself, man. What a devil ye are!
Now, let me tie you up for a while, for there are a dozen guns
trained on ye this minute."

Radison tried to speak, but could not; the reaction had seized him in that brief space, and he felt every ounce of strength leave him suddenly. He tried to raise his hand, saw Montenay reach out and take the knife from his nerveless fingers. Suddenly his knees gave way and he pitched forward into the snow.

He was unconscious for barely a minute, but when he woke was bound hand and foot. Bitterly cursing himself for that unexpected weakness, the result of the terrific strain, both mental and physical, that he had been under, he closed his eyes, while Montenay picked him up like a child and carried him in his arms to the lodge that he occupied.

As they passed Noreen's cabin he opened his eyes, but could see nothing of the girl, and with a little groan he surrendered himself to fate. Montenay carried him into the lodge and, placing him on the bed of fir-boughs and skins, built up the fire; then the giant departed without a word, lacing the caribou-skin door after him.

Dry-eyed, hopeless, Barr gazed up at the lodge-poles. It was all over now, he knew. Montenay had guessed his secret, and the giant would have no more mercy than would the Indians themselves. He shuddered slightly as there suddenly rose a long, piercing wail in a woman's voice. Then he got a grip on himself quickly. Where had the squaws come from?

Nichemus! The breed must have arrived with a party of the expected Chipewas while he and Montenay had been talking, of course. Then it was all over, and Montenay would win after all. Remembering Macklin, Barr's bloodless lips parted in a wolfish smile. At least, Montenay would not enjoy his triumph very long, and vengeance would be swift upon his trail.

"Lot of good that'll do me, though!" reflected Radison with a rueful grimace.

He lay motionless for hours, the thongs cutting off the circulation from his hands and feet, until at length he fell asleep from sheer weariness. His tremendous will-power had been flung out lavishly against Montenay and had conquered, but the effort was no light one, and followed as it had been by the fight in the shack, the result was utter and absolute exhaustion of body and soul.

When he awoke he saw that his fire had been banked with ashes, and that the night must have come. He could see no sign of food or water in the darkness, and everything seemed silent without. The attempt to change his position brought a groan of agony from him, for the thongs had cut down into his wrists.

A faint glow from his fire struck on the caribou-skin at the door, and after trying vainly to fall asleep once more, Radison stared wide-eyed before him, thinking bitterly on past events.

"Well, I guess I've got enough this time," he reflected. "If I could have gotten out of this with Noreen—oh, what's the use! I'll take what's coming to me, that's all."

Suddenly a tiny point of light directed his thoughts to Nichemus, whose parable of the star he had so wofully misunderstood. The little spark, reflecting the glow of the embers, moved slowly down the caribou-skin; a drop of water, melted from the rime outside, thought Radison.

He watched it roll down until it had passed out of the glow, then he started suddenly, for the caribou-hide had parted as if by magic, and into the lodge streamed a wild flare of crimson and purple, which betokened that the Spirit Dancers were in the heavens!

As he stared in dumb amazement he saw the ragged outlines of Yellow Wolf's flop-eared hood black against the sky, and the thought came to him that he was to be slain there as he lay helpless. Almost with the thought a whisper drifted to him.

"Strong Eyes! Is my brother awake?"

The voice was the voice of Uchichak.

CHAPTER XII

HANDICAPPED

"**D**ON'T STAND on ceremony, chief," Barr murmured with an almost hysterical laugh. "Come straight in—I'm awake all right."

A moment later a hand touched his mouth in token of silence, then the thongs about his ankles and wrists were severed. Barr lay incapable of motion until Uchichak brought snow and rubbed the chafed and swollen members; but at last, he made shift to stagger up, barely repressing a groan of agony and catching at the Indian for support.

"Is Macklin outside?"

The Crane shook his head, drawing the door-flap together.

"*Unnehoo!*" he breathed softly. "He brings bad luck on himself, my brother. When you can walk we must go quickly, for only squaws talk in an enemy's lodge."

Radison accepted the mild rebuke with a happy smile and peered through the caribou-skin severed by the Crane's knife. The village was seemingly deserted and was bathed in the weird glare from the sheeted figures who danced across the heavens and sent monstrous purple shadows careering over the snow. For a moment he listened to the hissing crackle and the deeper rumble of the lights, fantastically wondering why the stage machinery was not noiseless, then turned with a nod to Uchichak.

The other indicated that he wished to go first, and passed outside. Barr saw two pairs of snow-shoes stuck in the snow, and Uchichak slipped into one pair, of Chipewa make, handing Barr his own Ojibway shoes.

The American still wore his blanket capote and leggings, and his moccasins had saved his ankles from much harm, though the thongs had cut his wrists deeply. This was a small matter, however, and as Uchichak picked up his rifle Barr started off toward Noreen's shack. To his surprise, Uchichak grasped his shoulder roughly and halted him, pointing toward the cliffs.

"Got her out already?" whispered Barr. The Crane shook his head. "Well, we aren't going off without her, are we?"

Uchichak indicated assent, mingled with weary tolerance of the white man's vagaries. Barr hesitated, but he considered that the Crane must have some good reasons for such an action, and without more ado he gave in. No harm would come to Noreen for the present, and he had had more than one lesson that warned him not to force his will on these northmen unless he held the whip-hand over them.

So he followed Uchichak, muffled to the eyes, and speedily had proof that the camp was not left unguarded, and that it would have been risky in the extreme to attempt to get Noreen away with that sheeted fire of the Spirit Dancers overhead.

A dark figure sprang out of the ground, it seemed, with uncovered rifle.

"What cheer, what cheer!"

Uchichak calmly returned the greeting and spoke in Chipewa for a moment, after which the dark figure melted away and then went on. Radison was amazed at the ease of it, until he remembered that the Cree was wearing the garments of Yellow Wolf, and that with the large party which must have come in that day the sentinel was perhaps unsure of all the members.

This would account for Uchichak's pulling him through, and as he glanced at the many lodges which had been chinked with moss and skin-covered that day, he realized that Nichemus must have brought in a goodly contingent. There was a tingle in his raw knuckles as he thought of the breed, and with a grim laugh he wondered if his blow had broken Jean's jaw.

They left the village by a well-trodden trail, but no sooner had the first bushes closed around them than Uchichak halted and reversed his shoes, motioning to Barr to do the same. The American asked no questions, but obeyed the silent command, taking the gut-string handed him by the other and making a toe-loop of a single strand as Uchichak had done.

Now the Crane struck abruptly from the trail toward the cliffs to the south, making Barr go first in order to obliterate the tracks of the Ojibway shoes as much as possible. Although he was longing to question the other, Radison curbed himself, knowing that Uchichak would talk when he was ready to talk, and not an instant before.

The high cliffs, their black rock livened in the play of the Spirit Dancers, slowly rose above, and Radison saw that they were far west of the terrible cañon, and that Uchichak was scanning the dark rocks toward the place where Barr and Noreen had made such a disastrous attempt at escape.

There was none of the bare rock-edges under the cliffs at this point, and he two men sped along to the south-west, their grotesque shadows flickering on the rock wall beside them. They were striking up-wind, and suddenly the chief flung up his hood with a grunt of satisfaction. An instant later Barr caught a very faint drift of pine-smoke smell, and knew that they were almost at the journey's end. The high cliffs were filled with crannies and niches, caused by the snow-drippings of centuries, and he guessed that one of these held Uchichak's party.

Sure enough, a hundred yards farther on the chief turned him into a cranny of the crag, and he saw a huddle of dogs about a tiny fire, with a dark heap of furs at one side. A word from Uchichak quieted the dogs, and at the sound Barr saw the furs flung away, and he met the gaze of Macklin.

"Hello, old man! Sorry I can't shake, unless you lean over. How are you?"

"Mack!" Radison bent down, startled into swift anxiety at the sight of the Canadian's worn, parchmentlike features and the touch of the thin hand that gripped his. "Are you hurt? Why wouldn't the Crane talk? What's the matter?"

"Nothing much, now," and Macklin laughed faintly but

cheerfully. "We've lived on tea for three weeks, off and on, and tea is fine in its way, but makes a darned poor diet. Uchichak got a caribou three days ago, so we're all right. Hungry?"

"Mildly so," grinned Barr, and seeing that Uchichak was preparing a meal, he settled down beside Macklin and contentedly got out his pipe. The other grunted.

"Huh! Nice, clean little rip you got in the back! Weren't fool enough to take a chance on them Chipewa knives, were you?"

"Yep. Funeral in the village to-morrow, Tom. You tell your yarn first."

"Funeral? Good Lord, we're in bad all around, Rad! You know what happened at Murphy's? Well, Uchichak and I saw you pile into Montenay's gang and get laid out cold, then we went back and found Murphy dead with a Chipewa in his arms, crushed.

"Next morning came the chief's son, Pekoos, with word that the warriors could not arrive for two weeks. We sent the Sandfly back to bring them ahead, and Uchichak told the young fellow to fetch 'em by Montenay's trail, describing the straight pass through the hills by which you prob'ly got in.

"Well, the chief tells me there's a long trail ahead, and if we cuts corners we might cross the hills by another way and beat Montenay here. So I says to take a chance on it."

"We got into the hills right enough, but blamed if we could get out! The chief got balled up worse'n a husky in his first harness, and one night we got careless with our stuff and a cussed wolverine played merry halleluiah with all our grub, leaving only the tea, on account of the dogs smelling him too late.

"Well, that was mighty bad, and we got in a heap worse, for we couldn't pull out and we couldn't go ahead, just a wandering and meandering in a casual sort of way. Add to that, a couple of days later I went over the side of a cliff, busted my blooming ankle and a rib or so, and the Crane had to break trail after that.

"Then we just starved, Barr. After a week of berries and bark,

Uchichak spoke of eating the dogs, but you know, maybe, what he thinks of them dogs! Anyway, we concluded the dogs were too skinny, and if we ate 'em I'd be stuck there for good, so we starved and they starved. Jumping sandhills, but that was a lonely time!

"A week ago we struck your trail—at least, the chief said it was yours and that you had a girl with you, from the sign. So we trailed along till another fellow joined you, and it finally brought us out on the cliffs, with a little path leading down here.

"Well, to cut it short, the chief said he'd take a chance on getting you out of the village so you could help with taking care o' me, but it'd be foolishness to get the girl."

Radison nodded slowly, disappointment heavy upon him.

"Where are the Crees, then?" he asked. "How did Uchichak get Yellow Wolf's outfit?"

"As to the outfit, Yellow Wolf dropped in on us yesterday, which was a mighty bad thing for him to do. Anyhow, he don't need the outfit to keep him warm now," Macklin chuckled to himself. "We haven't had a smell o' the Crees, Rad; but the chief found that Montenay doesn't keep any watch to speak of."

At this juncture Uchichak snatched the caribou steaks from the fire and Radison was soon at work, relating his own story while he ate. The Cree asked several questions as to the personnel of the Chipewa party, but Macklin heard the tale in unconcealed amazement.

"Fight the company, will he? I guess your friend Montenay is going to be in darned hot water before he gets through, Rad. It—well, spit it out, Uchichak!"

The chief had risen uneasily, and now he spoke quickly and with his usual decision:

"Talking Owl is a great warrior. He and Nichemus will follow us here, my brothers; and this is no good place. Let us go back to the top of the cliffs and camp."

"That's right," added Macklin hastily. "It's long past midnight,

Barr. They'll find out about your escape as soon as the camp begins to wake up, so we'd better beat it."

Uchichak began packing caribou meat on the sled, but Radison sat thinking swiftly. Even should they reach the crest of the cliffs, they would be in poor shape for holding off the Chipewas. But could they once get back to the mouth of that notch in the crags through which Montenay passed on his mysterious errands, it could be held against an army.

He quickly put the situation before the others. If the Crees were on the way to their assistance, and were coming by way of that wind-lashed pass, then it was doubly necessary for them to gain the mouth of the pass and hold it. Uchichak realized the strategical importance of the move in a flash.

"*Miwasin!* Let us go quickly. Strong Eyes, take the rifle of Wakinakun."

"Me!" chuckled Macklin in response to Barr's puzzled look. "The Juniper, in other words. The Jibways call me Running Moose, as you heard down south."

Radison nodded with a smile, and, to tell the truth, both names were appropriate to the rangy Canadian. Suddenly, as he was helping Macklin aboard the sled, a thought struck him.

"You got hurt before you got out of the hills, you say?"

"Years ago, seems like."

"Uchichak! Let's see your *muskisinew!* Are you wearing flat-shoes?"

For answer the chief raised a foot and showed a regular moccasin of one-piece sole. Barr was frankly puzzled, and stared from one to the other.

"Yesterday," he explained, "Noreen and I found a flat shoe-print in the snow under the cliffs, near the gorge. None of the Chipewas wore them, and I thought it was made by you, Mack. But if you haven't been able to move, and Uchichak doesn't wear 'em—"

He paused, and for once detected a trace of blank surprise on the bronzed features of the Crane. However, he realized that this was no time to ponder over the mystery, so he dismissed the subject with a laugh.

"Come along—maybe it was the ghost! We'll have to hustle to reach; that cañon; so get those brutes of yours harnessed up, chief."

Uchichak took his whip, but the five half-wild dogs needed only his voice to subdue them, and in ten minutes the aching and weary but thoroughly happy American was breaking trail beneath the cliffs.

The only fly in the ointment of his satisfaction was the fact that Noreen was still a prisoner. When he had mentioned her name Macklin had flung him one whimsical glance, and Barr smiled quietly at thought of the confession which must be forthcoming sooner or later.

The Spirit Dancers were flinging gaunt shapes of living flame far across the heavens, and the way lay clear before him. Searching the bleak line of crags, Radison figured that they had only two or three miles to cover at most before reaching the gorge, and his heart was eager within him.

He held the trail close to the cliffs, over deep-drifted snow that was untouched from year to year by the far southern sun, and across the silent night each faintest sound boomed echo from the iron rocks above.

Suddenly the American started as if the Crane's snake-whip had lashed him. Up through the far trees, sharp and shrill on the frosted air, rose a single quavering yell. So terrible was the sound of it, so athrill with the blood-lust of savagery, that for an instant Barr's blood ran cold.

"*Mash, mash!*" rang out the Crane's voice from behind, followed by Macklin's startled cry.

"Hit out, Rad! They're after us!"

The American set his teeth and swung forward to the work in grim silence. His confidence had been shattered in a second, and as he peered ahead through the frost-rime that edged his hood he felt something very akin to dismay swell up in him, for the gorge must be a good mile away still.

A moment later Uchichak, handing the whip to Macklin, surged ahead of Barr with a rush and fled over the snow into the nearest trees like some wraith of the forest. Barr knew instinctively that the chief would scout along beside them to ward off possible danger, and, urging every aching muscle to the task, he plunged forward in a terrific spurt, while Macklin kept the long lash snapping over the huskies behind.

"If we can't make it, Rad, jump ahead—they won't hurt me!" cried the Canadian.

"Go to the devil!" flung back Radison angrily, and he heard Macklin chuckle despite the situation. His eyes searched the line of cliffs, and now the ledges of black rock, interspersed with huge fragments split from the granite cliffs, drew near on his right. As he swung out slightly to avoid the windswept surfaces he uncased his rifle; the frost might cause the weapon to burst, but he must not be taken unawares at this juncture.

One more long yell, swift and sharp and snappy this time, rang over the barrens, and he knew the Chipewas were on the trail. Now the notch in the cliffs was visible, still a half mile away; and even as he made it out Barr saw a shade dart from the trees and swing out to meet him at an angle. Uchichak came up amid a cloud of snow-dust, his rifle also bared.

"Nichemus, Talking Owl, and twenty braves!" panted the chief as he ran. "They are coming this way to search along the cliff—they will see us!"

"Get in among the rocks, you two," ordered Macklin sharply. "What's that ahead? Swing into that angle, Rad—quick!"

Barr obeyed instantly. A huge fragment of rock, fifty feet high and a hundred long, had been ripped away from the main cliff; in between lay a narrow passage a dozen feet wide, open at each end and carpeted with snow. Macklin's quick eye had caught its possibilities at once, and the near opening was but fifty feet away.

Racing forward, barely a foot ahead of the dogs, Radison suddenly felt a broken upthrust of the snow-crust strike the edge of his shoe, and he lost his stride for a bare instant. Before he could draw away the leading husky had overrun his shoes, and he plunged down in a mad whirl of snapping, excited dogs that piled up on top of him.

Cursing furiously at his lack of caution, he flung them off, arms over his face to protect it from the wolfish teeth. Uchichak charged down into the midst and helped him up, but the evil was done.

One wild burst of yells went up from the line of trees below, a dozen little spats of flame shot out, and Barr heard a *zip* overhead; then Macklin's hand seemed to leap into a spout of fire and the tearing *r-r-r-rip* of an automatic split the air, while Uchichak frantically drove the dogs onward.

Dark figures appeared at the edge of the trees as Barr gained the rock shelter. He turned and raised his rifle. A glance over his shoulder showed him Uchichak, now at the far end of the narrow passage, slashing at the traces of the dogs with his knife. For a quick instant Barr wondered; but lead splattered on the rock behind him, and he dropped to one knee, took careful aim, and fired.

CHAPTER XIII

THE MAN OF PEACE

THE ATTACK ceased as abruptly as it had begun. The Spirit Dancers flared down upon two motionless forms in the snow, and the rest had broken back to the cover of the trees, which afforded excellent shelter.

Barr had caught no sign of Nichemus, though the voice of the breed had rung high above the others, but as a dropping fire sent the rock-splinters singing about him he drew back and turned to meet Uchichak, who held his rifle in one hand and the dog-whip in the other, the huskies whining at his heels.

The American glanced past Uchichak at the figure of Macklin, sitting up on the shed, and an idea flashed into his brain.

"Watch here," he said quickly. "They can't get across that open space, but they could go around well enough, or cut over to the shelter of the rocks farther back and then sweep this place with a raking fire. I'm going down here for a look."

Uchichak nodded, and without hesitation Barr ran for the other end of the passage. During his walks with Noreen he had noted that from a little distance this whole line of cliffs appeared one unbroken mass, and now it occurred to him that it might be possible for them to draw the sled onward through the scattered rocks, protected from the muskets of the Chipewas, before the latter knew that the shelter was deserted.

Passing Macklin with a reassuring word, the American reached the opposite end of the passage, and could not repress a cry of exultation. Doubtless by the same cataclysm which had slithered off the first mass of rock, it seemed that an entire section had been torn away in huge blocks for nearly the whole length of the cliffs.

The great crags towered far above on the right, and on the left were the jagged fifty-foot fragments in an almost continuous line. Radison turned to the anxious Canadian and quickly outlined his plan.

"Even if they do catch on, Mack, we'll have enough start to reach the gorge. That place is a bare ten feet across at the bottom, and we can hold it as long as we have cartridges."

"Go get the Crane—we'll take a chance," answered Macklin cheerily.

Hastening away, Barr wondered why Uchichak had cut the dog-traces. Splicing them again would mean delay, and now every moment counted, for the peculiar rock formation must be known to some of the Chipewas.

Uchichak was coolly standing and emptying his magazine, bullets singing around him, when Barr pulled him back. The chief smiled and wiped a smear of half-frozen blood from his cheek, but his eyes lit up at the American's explanation, which he understood readily. Much of his English had deserted him in the excitement, and he spoke in a deep, guttural tone that Barr had not heard from him before.

"*Miwasin!* These Chipewa squaws cannot shoot, and we do it good. You wait—mebbe—"

His speech was broken into by a swift half-dozen spurts of flame a hundred yards distant, directly under the cliffs and in line with them. Barr felt something tug at his shoulder, saw the chief's hood fly back, and dragged the Cree down into shelter.

What he most dreaded had happened. Nichemus, with his magazine-rifle, was more to be feared than all the Chipewa muskets.

That first volley had bespoken the deadliness of his aim, for between the rocks and the cliff proper there was shadow, yet only by chance had the two men escaped. Uchichak had a slight scalp-wound, and the shoulder of Radison's capote was torn away, and the American made no bones about dashing back to Macklin before Nichemus could reload.

He seized the dog-whip and was about to get the harness in order when Uchichak stopped him. Reaching down, the Cree uncoiled a length of knotted hide fastened to the sled and nodded to Barr to catch hold. The American obeyed, and now for the first time he perceived what the cunning Indian had intended from the start.

Taking the five dogs to the sled, Uchichak spoke to them in his own tongue, and led them behind a sheltering jog in the wall. His gestures, the lolling tongues of the wolfish huskies, their low growls and bristling necks, all these told the world-old story of man bidding the dumb brutes who loved him to serve him to the death.

Leaving the huskies with a leap, Uchichak seized the tug-rope and flung his weight upon it. The light sled darted forward through the opening, and just in time; a hail of bullets came sweeping down the narrow passage, one or two crashing through the frail sled, while another smashed the heel of Barr's right shoe as he dragged it on the snow. They lunged forward unharmed, however, and were gone at a run.

Radison did not look back. He heard a chorus of wild yells that spurred him on, and for a moment the echoing swish of snow-shoes drove down the passageway. Suddenly this was lost in a burst of vicious snarls, and the American shuddered as over the tumult rose the wolfish cry of the kill— *"Yap! Yap! Yap—gur-r-rr."*—and one horrible man-scream that rang in his ears for days. The Crane was well served.

From his sled Macklin turned and sent a string of ten bullets into the seething mass of men and dogs behind. The American heard no answering shots, and knowing that the Chipewas had probably emptied their muzzle-loaders, could well imagine what that struggle of steel against teeth was like.

The fieldlike yells of the Indians were increased tenfold by the rocks and swelled in rolling bursts along the crags. Then the yapping growls died away, somewhere a musket crashed out—and Barr was pulling the sled alone.

"Go!" panted Uchichak hoarsely. "I hold 'em—go quick—quick!"

Radison did not stop to argue, but dragged himself forward, the hide-rope cutting into his shoulder where the capote was torn away, his smashed shoe trailing almost useless.

He dimly heard Macklin storming at him to go on alone and leave the sled, but this was drowned by the barking reports of Uchichak's rifle, and into his brain pierced the shrill war-cry of the chief.

All but winded, he strained for sight of that notch in the cliffs as silence fell behind him, and quickly found the place. Would he ever reach it? The American summoned up every ounce of his reserve energy, and with locked teeth swung ahead.

He did not know that he was reeling blindly as he ran; that Macklin was making frenzied efforts to loosen the thongs that held him to the sled; to fling himself off and so force the American to go on alone. He did know that with a tremendous surge of relief he felt strong hands catch the rope behind him and lift the burden; out of the tail of his eye he glimpsed a tall figure and shouted his relief.

"Good boy, Uchichak! I thought—you were—staying—all done—"

He caught his breath and plunged forward, the mouth of the gorge in sight. Remembering that the Chipewas must be catching up, he dropped the rope and staggered aside, fumbling to reload his rifle with mittened hands.

"Go ahead—it's my turn to hold them, Uchichak."

He raised the weapon. As the mists cleared away from before his eyes and the passage took shape, he was surprised to see it empty, save for a number of dark forms that writhed in the snow or lay quiet. Abruptly he perceived his mistake as muskets flashed out, two hundred yards behind, and from somewhere closer at hand cracked a rifle.

"That's funny—they don't seem to be shooting at me!" he muttered, standing and staring down the passage. "What's happened, anyhow? I wonder if Montenay's down the line there? Hope the brute got his from those dogs!"

With which charitable wish he emptied his magazine at the flashes and jerked out the shells. Raising the weapon again he waited until the rifle of Nichemus began its spiteful volley, and was just pressing the trigger when a hand fell on his shoulder.

"Come—and quickly!"

Radison whirled, for the voice was that of a white man, but unknown to him. The figure told him nothing. It was tall and ragged of outline, white from head to foot with frost-rime and snow-spume, but the man carried no weapon. Where was Uchichak? The thought was answered by a shot and the Cree battle-cry from down the passage.

"Who are you?" demanded the astounded American, springing back, every nerve on edge.

"A friend—what else would I be helping you with Macklin for? Turn that gun off me and walk along, you wild divil, you! Do you want to be murdering the chief? Hurry!"

Dazed, Radison lowered his rifle.

"But who in—was it you who grabbed the rope?"

"Botheration—I've not time to be chattering here like an old woman at a wedding!"

A hand of iron closed on Radison's arm and he was dragged after the tall figure until he ran in half-angry bewilderment at its side. In a moment the dark entrance of the pass rose before them, the giant crags towering sheer up on either hand, and the inner passageway brought them just inside the entrance itself.

Radison looked about for Macklin as his guide stopped short. To one side lay the sled, splintered and broken, a shapeless mass of wood; but of the Canadian there was no sign. Then he saw that the tall figure had stooped and was rising with a rifle hanging over one arm.

"Now wait here," came the sharp order, "for I must get Uchichak, and we may be needin' you to cover us. But mind— don't be emptying that gun promiscuous down our way! Here, take this one of mine, for you may have to shoot fast."

"But you?" cried Barr as the other pressed the spare weapon into his hands and turned. "You aren't going back there unarmed?"

"I'm a man of peace, my son," came the reply, and the figure flitted away at a run, seeming to vanish suddenly into the air.

Barr rubbed his clean rime-edged hood and stared—then gave a little laugh. The tall figure was covered with powdery snow and rime, so that at a short distance it merged absolutely with the snow, especially under the flickering shadow-play of the Dancers.

So Uchichak was still holding off the Chipewas—but who

was this amazing friend, who called himself a man of peace, yet possessed a grip like living steel? Again Barr glanced around for Macklin, but though the tracks passed down into the hundred-yard straight-away that led to the first twist in the gorge, he could see nothing but the sheer black walls all about, and with a queer sense of oppression he turned to the task in hand.

Now the Spirit Dancers seemed to be leaving the stage, and gloom had settled gradually upon the passage under the cliffs. One or two guns spat fire, and Radison caught the sharper crack of a rifle, though he could make out no figures of men.

He waited, rifle ready, and once more the thought of Montenay filled him with uneasiness. It was not like the giant to leave pursuit to the Chipewas, yet he had caught no echo of the rolling bass voice through all the tumult.

"Ping-g-g!"

A bullet drove past him with eager whine and spattered on the rock wall. Slowly a vague something took form in the obscurity ahead, a grotesque shape, monstrous and unhuman, and in swift, unreasoning panic Radison flung up his rifle.

"Easy, you wild American!"

With the biting words Barr saw what that outlandish figure was. The tall man of peace was striding toward him, bearing on his shoulders the figure of Uchichak, and Radison stepped forward with a throb of relief. The gloom of the place, the tremendous cliffs above and around him, had unnerved him for a moment.

"Is Uchichak hurt?"

"That depends," and the stranger lowered the body to the snow with a grunt. "I've known people to say that bullets hurt, and I've known 'em say that nothing *can* hurt, so you may just take your choice. Now, is it wanting to start a discussion you are, or would you suggest seeking shelter?"

Radison laughed half angrily and shot a look down the gloom of the passage.

"For a man of peace, my friend, you have a decidedly vitriolic tongue! However, I'm too done up to argue. Go ahead and finish your rescue-work since you seem pretty keen on the job. I'll surrender!"

The other chuckled, stooped over Uchichak, and carried the chief a dozen feet away, around the corner of the cañon entrance. Barr followed, pausing abruptly at sight of a dark mass coming along the snow of the narrow passageway. Again his rifle went up, and again the man of peace halted him quickly, this time with a tense whisper.

"Wait! Oh, you murderin' villain, will you go slow? In here, for your life!"

The viselike grip seized and flung him toward the projecting corner of the cliff, and the bewildered Radison obeyed blindly. He seemed to be moving in some wild nightmare, through which flitted the mysterious man of peace like one of the ghostly Spirit Dancers come to earth.

His brain cleared in a moment. Watching with mittened finger on trigger in spite of his orders, he was amazed to see the tall stranger calmly pause in the center of the passage where it turned into the mouth of the gorge. The white-spumed figure stood silent, arms folded, like some weird frost-shape; Barr saw that where Uchichak had rubbed the whiteness from his shoulders the man had dusted more of the powdered snow.

Slowly the dark mass down the passage resolved itself into the cautiously advancing forms of the Chipewas. Overhead where the sky seemed to clamp down on the iron cliffs, fitful flickerings battled against the unfading southern sunlight, and what little light filtered down into the passage was a dim, greenish radiance that ebbed and flooded without giving coherent vision.

So it was, perhaps, that for a long moment the advancing Chipewas did not see the white figure in the snow. Watching in dread anxiety, Barr put down a hand to check a movement of the reviving Cree chief, and at the same instant he caught a swift motion of the tall stranger, who flung the hood back from his head and started forward to meet the Chipewas.

To the stupefaction of the watching American, not an Indian raised a weapon, but the dark figures stood as if frozen to their shoes. During the brief minute that followed the air seemed charged with some subtle force, some electrical tensity that sent Radison forward on his toes; then he caught a low, spreading whisper of sheer horror that swelled and surged up into a yell of terror—and the Chipewas were gone.

Instantly the man of peace went to his knees, gathered up snow, and began rubbing it over his face and ears with fierce energy. The common-sense action awoke Radison from his almost superstitious fixity. There was nothing supernatural about a person who feared the deadly frost-bite, at all events! He felt his hand gripped by Uchichak, and the Cree dragged himself up unsteadily.

"Where is my brother the Juniper? Is Uchichak in the spirit-world?"

"Darned near it, I guess," returned Barr slowly. "Are you wounded, chief?"

"A little," and the Crane staggered out into the passage. He was stopped by the man of peace, who drew up his hood and rose. A few words in Cree were exchanged, Barr heard a startled cry from Uchichak, and was amazed to see the grim chief go to his knees. The white figure exclaimed impatiently and pulled him up.

"Radison, the chief wants his rifle—we left it down there. Give him mine, will you?"

Barr stepped forward and obeyed, then turned on the stranger.

"Look here, my peaceful friend, I'd like to have an explanation of all this. I'm no child, and you sure get on my nerves. Now let's have something solid for a change. Where's Tom Macklin, and who are you?"

Uchichak broke into excited speech, but the other stopped him.

"Sufficient unto the day is the evil thereof, my young dare-devil! Don't be gazing at me now, but thank the good God that I came in time to save you from yourself—Lord bless you, what a poor, misguided man o' muscle it is! Come along and I'll satisfy you that I'm the best friend who ever stepped out to your assistance, no less! All ready, Uchichak? Can you walk?"

The chief nodded, and the tall stranger, taking Barr's arm, turned him toward the darkness of the gulch with a low chuckle that held no mirth in it.

CHAPTER XIV

CRAZY BEAR TRAPPED

SO UTTERLY spent was Barr Radison by the flight from the village and the events which had followed that he gave himself up uncomplainingly to the will of this commanding stranger.

As they passed the shattered sled Uchichak, leaning heavily on his rifle, the stranger slashed at the thongs and loaded himself with what was left of the caribou meat.

Radison wondered dully if he was going to lead them down into that horrible gorge where the wind was roaring and whistling, and it seemed that he was doing so. Who could this man be? Not the Pierre Radisson of Montenay's fantastic talk, certainly, although the very idea sent a cold shiver crawling up Barr's back.

"Nonsense!" he collected himself with an angry effort. "This foolishness is going to end mighty sudden, once we get out of here. If I wasn't sick of this eternal scrapping I'd put it up to him pretty strong. Guess he's some strong-jawed chap himself, but he can't put that stuff over me!"

He guessed that the other was Irish by the slight touch of brogue in the rich, hard voice that had bitten through the frost with the ring of authority; but aside from this there was no clue.

The gorge, as Radison had seen the day that he followed Montenay, lay between the straight, sheer walls for a hundred yards, then went twisting and twining through the hills beyond, cloaked in the blackness of the earth-deeps.

Their guide led them almost to the end of the stretch, following a trail that seemed well beaten into the snow, and Barr wondered how the man had carried Macklin for that distance as he must have done. A moment afterward they were halted, and with a gesture their guide kicked free of his snow-shoes.

Obeying that gesture, Radison looked up at the wall on his right. A yard above his head, with an ascent of fallen rock leading up to it, stretched a high, narrow cleft in the sheer crag—silent, black, grim, with unsensed terrors.

Remembering how Montenay had suddenly vanished, Barr knew at once that here was the solution of the problem, in this cave that lay a gash in the granite cliff.

"Matches?" inquired the man of peace laconically. "I left my fire-bag inside."

As Barr carried his matches in a fire-bag at his waist, Indian fashion, he soon had them out and handed them to the stranger, who refused them.

"Those Chipewas won't hang fire very long, Radison, so I'll be going back for a bit. Now mind what I'm tellin' you! Go straight in and get to sleep, for I'm fearing there'll be a stiff time ahead.

"Montenay's in there, and I'll leave it to you to tie him up, not havin' the time myself. It's drunk he is, and helpless, so don't dare slip your knife into him, Uchichak, or I'll make you sweat for it, my son. One word, Radison! Is the little maid safe an' well?"

"Who—Noreen?" blurted out Radison, surprised. The other

nodded. "Why, she was well enough this morning—or yesterday morning, rather, when I last saw her."

"God bless her! 'Tis not the likes of Montenay will iver hurt
her! Now run along with you, and peace be on the bloody hands
of the both o' you!"

Uchichak bowed his head, and the stranger's hands touched
his hood for an instant, but Barr was too weary to remain longer,
and staggered up the broken rock ascent to the cave. Reaching
the entrance he caught the hand of Uchichak and helped him
to climb painfully up, a glance showing him that the tall man
of peace had vanished. In another moment Barr had stripped
off a mitten, lit a match, and stared ahead.

The cave consisted of a narrow passage some twenty feet
high, and two yards from the entrance there was a sharp bend.
Reaching this, Barr found another beyond, and another, while
Uchichak muttered wearily about the Spirit Dancers living in
such a place as this.

As the match flickered out Barr paused in the act of lighting
a second, for the winding passage ahead was lit with a faint
glow of light. Remembering that Macklin was no doubt here,
he raised his voice.

"Mack! Are you here?"

"Hello, Barr! Come right ahead, and get a move on. Montenay's getting uneasy."

Mindful of the stranger's words, Radison pushed ahead and
finally issued into a widening of the passage which formed a
small chamber, a dozen feet across and twice as long.

The place was lit and warmed by a small fire, beside which
lay Macklin, his hood thrown back and his automatic close to
his hand. Against one wall were piled a dozen small kegs, while
the whole floor of the place was deep with skins, several bundles
being piled in a corner. Half stretched out on these, near a large
opening at the rear of the cave, was Montenay, breathing heavily,
while a reek of liquor in the air betrayed his condition.

"Tie him up, Rad!" exclaimed Macklin excitedly. "The game's

in our hands or I'm a Dutchman! Who's the fellow that carried me here? Must be strong as a bull!"

"Never saw him before," returned Barr, kneeling beside Montenay and cutting a strip from one of the pelts on the floor. With this he bound the giant's hands, then his ankles, and straightened up with a sigh of relief. Uchichak had sunk down by the fire, and Barr shook him anxiously.

"Here, chief! Where are you wounded? Reach over and give me a hand with his capote, Tom—there, that's better. Glory be, what a head!"

Uchichak got to his feet, his iron frame completely given out, and when Macklin told him that the chief had not slept for three nights Radison did not wonder. The Crane's head and neck were streaming with blood, melted in the warmth of the chamber, while he had a ripping tear across one cheek and a bullet had broken the skin for the full width of his chest, but without much damage.

None of his wounds were serious, and after exploring his capote, Barr found some sticking-plaster, the universal Indian remedy, and as there was no other bandage to be had, he applied this and let the Crane sink back, sound asleep.

"I'm off," he murmured drowsily, stretched out on the profusion of skins near Macklin. "Other man's watching, Tom—go to sleep, old chap—"

With which he knew nothing more than that Macklin muttered some response which was lost in the infinity of slumber. It had not been very long since he had lain in his lodge and seen that moving point of light roll down the caribou hide; but even then he had been weary, and the time between had been crowded with incident and labor.

Whoever the man of peace might be, he was at least highly concerned with defeating Montenay, and that was quite enough for Radison just at present.

He was wakened by a rough shaking and opened his eyes

with a groan of protest to gaze up at a face that struck him silent with awe and wonder.

High of brow, with dead black hair, the face was disfigured by a twisting scar which wiped off half the left eyebrow in a red smear; below, deep-set black eyes flamed with virile power and in spite of the ragged black beard Radison could see that the close-lipped mouth, hollow cheeks, and square, bony jaw denoted tremendous determination and strength of character.

Barr lay watching while the man wakened Macklin and Uchichak in turn, and knew that this must be their mysterious helper.

His capote had been flung off, and he was clothed in tattered remnants of cloth mingled with rudely fashioned fur garments. Glancing at the capote by the fire, Radison saw that it was worn to shreds and patched with skin.

The caribou meat brought from the sled load thawed out, and strips of it were sizzling over the fire with an odor that brought the newly aroused men to their feet, save Macklin, who sat up sniffing ravenously.

While the Crane squatted over the fire, fishing for his pipe and tobacco, Radison and Macklin stared at the stranger, who paid them no heed, but picked up his capote and threw it on. At the entrance to the passage he turned suddenly.

"I'll be back soon—it's nearly noon now. Nichemus and the Chipewas have camped down just outside the mouth of the pass, and seem to be waiting for Montenay to turn up before they attack. Whatcheer!"

The tall figure vanished, and Radison stared at Macklin for a moment until he recollected that Uchichak had recognized the stranger the night before. He turned to the chief with an eager question, and Uchichak slowly removed the pipe from his lips and replied in a matter-of-fact tone:

"Père Sulvent."

"Sulvent!"

The cry came from Radison and Macklin together. A flicker

of amusement brought out the crow's-feet around the eyes of the Crane, but he stared steadily at the hissing caribou-steaks, puffing away in stolid content that all was well for the moment.

"But we thought he was dead!" exclaimed Barr, looking for a moment at Montenay, who still snored away in his corner. "Montenay said himself that he had killed him, Uchichak— there must be some mistake, surely!" The Crane's beady eyes shifted suddenly to the form of Montenay, and a hand dropped to the ready knife, but the impulse was restrained instantly and he answered with stolid indifference, rising to his feet:

"I know *le bon père,* my brothers. There is no mistake. When I saw his face last night my heart was like water, for I thought him a ghost. How this thing has happened I know not—I know not—but—but—"

The two others stared at him as his voice died away. The beady eyes were looking down, the man stood as if frozen stiff, and his whole attitude expressed a stupefied incredulity that was little short of fear.

"What's the matter?" cried Macklin in alarm, while Radison stepped forward quickly. For answer the Cree pointed down.

"Is the Crane bewitched by the hill-devils?" came the hoarse, thick words. "Look—*Kusketawukases!*" An inarticulate cry broke from Macklin, while Barr stared down, less impressed than the others. The Canadian caught up an armful of the pelts in wild excitement.

"You're dead right, chief—black fox, every one! Here's a silver fox—Great Scott, Barr! Do you realize that we're right on top of a fortune, with black fox selling at a thousand a skin?"

Radison nodded, but did not stoop to gather up the wonderful furs at his feet. After a minute he turned to Macklin with a thin-lipped smile, touching Uchichak's shoulder as he did so.

"The Crane thinks so much of pelts that he lets the meat burn; but not all these furs put together could buy us more meat."

An exclamation broke from Uchichak, and he dropped the

pelts, while Macklin looked up and met the American's eyes. Montenay's sodden snores sounded loud.

"Huh? What do you mean, Rad?"

"What I say. That meat on the fire, with the other few chunks, is all we have. Think it over while I get some snow."

Taking a copper tea-pail that stood in the corner, Barr left by the winding passage and soon stood in the opening above the cañon. There was no sign of life around. A faint light from far above showed him that it was indeed daylight, and he descended to the snow. Here were Uchichak's snow-shoes and his own, and taking his shattered right shoe he dug through the hard crust and packed the copper pail with snow.

Gaining the cave again, he looked back at the cleft, something on the smooth rock wall catching his eye. Striking a match, he made out words rudely painted on the rock, and smiled as he recognized a verse of Montenay's "luck"—the old pirate song that had sounded so incongruous here in the frozen north.

"I suppose he painted that in one of his drunken moods," reflected Barr. "He must have been pretty larried to spell as badly as this. Funny he didn't seem to know the tune, though!"

He returned to find Uchichak and Macklin gravely discussing their situation, with all thought of the pelts forgotten for the present. Hanging the tea-pail on the stick over the fire, Radison helped them to dispose of the cooked meat, after which it was decided that the remainder should be made ready for Sulvent.

"He looked rather hungry himself," stated Macklin curiously. "He's done enough for us to deserve a feed, I guess; anyhow, it's better to have one good feed and take a chance on getting another than it is to starve by inches."

"I'm willing," returned Barr. "You see, Mack, we're practically hemmed in here. We can't get out to the woods to pick up anything, and the only other course is to hit right back along the cañon, which we wouldn't dare attempt without dogs or food, for there's no game."

"Well, we've got *him*," and Macklin jerked a thumb at the recumbent Montenay. "I guess those Chipewas are educated out of their fear of the company, Rad, and now that we've dropped some of them there'll be no peace. Otherwise two or three of these skins would fetch 'em around. This fellow Montenay live here or at the village?"

"Both, it seemed. He had a shack there, but comes over here half the time to get drunk. Why?"

"Because he ought to have some grub here—go to it, chief! You've got the right idea," added the Canadian as Uchichak rose and looked about searchingly, with a contemptuous glance at Montenay. "Well, we have this fellow nailed down, that's one comfort. Might use him as a hostage, Barr!"

Radison related his conversation with Montenay in regard to the Chipewas, while the Crane investigated the contents of the chamber.

"No," he concluded gravely, "I'm afraid that his influence is a matter of muscle. I don't know what those Silent Ones are he talks about, but it's a cinch he'll get a bad jolt when he wakes up to find Père Sulvent here. That's a mighty queer thing, Tom! Even the factor and McShayne swore that Sulvent was dead."

"Well, we can take a chance on the Sandfly getting here with the Crees," returned the Canadian. "If that's really Sulvent, they say he could twist the Crees around his little finger, and he might be able to get 'em here quick. Find anything, chief?"

Uchichak had brought one of the little kegs into the light of the fire, and shook it, smelling. He flung it away with a gesture of disgust.

"*Iskootawapoo!* Fire-liquor—bah!"

"The chief hasn't much use for whisky," laughed Macklin. "See what's in the rest of the kegs, Uchichak."

One by one the Cree brought out the little kegs and examined them. Only two contained liquor, and, setting the others aside, Uchichak tried to open one with his knife, but could not. Radison had seen an ax with the copper pail, and procuring this he stove in the head of the little keg. It contained nothing but powder, and he did not bother to open the others.

"Pisisik—nothing else," grunted Uchichak, and his eyes roved to the opening at the far end of the chamber. "What is that?"

Radison shrugged his shoulders and pulled out his pipe, for he had no hope that there was any food stored here. With all the curiosity of a child the Crane took a brand from the fire and approached the opening.

"Well," said Barr as he settled down at Macklin's side, "I wish our friend, the dead priest, would return to explain his mystery. We'll get Montenay's out of him, all right—he'll be so scared when he sees Sulvent that he'll give up all he knows—"

He was cut short by a low, terrible moan from the opening where the Crane had disappeared, and back into the chamber staggered the chief, his eyes rolling and his face ashen gray.

"The Spirit Dancers! The Spirit Dancers—in there!" he gasped, and as the two men stared at him he reeled and fled down the entrance way.

CHAPTER XV

SULVENT'S TALE

"STOP HIM, Rad!" Macklin half rose and fell back with a groan. "What's up?"

"Search me," and Barr stared with startled eyes at the opening. They both knew that no ordinary thing would so terrify Uchichak, and without a word Macklin handed up his automatic. Nothing appeared in the opening, however, and Barr was just reaching for his matches when he was startled by a laugh from Montenay.

"So Uchichak found the Silent Ones, eh?"

Whirling, he saw the giant staring from his corner, wide awake. He had evidently taken in the situation in a flash and resigned himself to it, for now he was the Montenay whom Radison rather liked, after a fashion.

"Well, I see ye've got me, Radisson; though I'm cursed if I know how ye found the place! I was a fool to doubt the prophecy."

"What's in there?" cried Barr. "What prophecy do you mean?"

"Easy, man; easy! If ye want to see the prophecy reach in and get the paper out o' my capote—there's a pocket in the breast. Who helped you out of the lodge—Uchichak? Aye, it must ha' been a regular Cree trick!"

Radison handed back the automatic to Macklin and strode across the chamber. Bending over the giant he loosened the shaggy bearskin capote and felt inside the breast, while Montenay looked up into his eyes with a slight smile. Drawing out a paper, he crossed back to the fire and settled down beside Macklin, who peered over his shoulder.

The paper was old, ragged, and seemed to be the last of other sheets, for at the top it was numbered in Roman. Glancing at the faded writing, Radison saw with sudden interest that it was done by the same hand which had autographed the old Bible— doubtless that of Radisson himself, though there was no signature and the writing broke off abruptly as it began.

XXXI

—shall beware how you doe deal with my Truste. In Time shall come Them of Mine owne Race, nay of mine owne Name, & to Them doe I Pierre Radisson graunt all Things. The faithful Brethren of the 5 Nations are dead & butt the Keeper & Swift Arrow live. God bless my childn. for I doe grow weak & in this new Land there be no game to—

Barr looked up, wonder in his eyes.

"That's all," he said simply. "Is this what you call a prophecy, Montenay?"

"Is it not prophecy enough, man?"

"It's wonderful!" broke in Macklin. "Let's have a glom of it, old man—to think Pierre Radisson wrote this himself! Where'd you get it, Montenay?"

"From him," chuckled the giant with a roar of laughter at the amazed look of the Canadian. Macklin looked over the paper, and was handing it back when Barr saw Montenay's face change, the laughter died into a choking gurgle, and with one horrible cry the man fell back motionless.

A shuffling of moccasins and Radison whirled to see Père Sulvent standing in the doorway, hood flung back, and one hand gripping the shoulder of Uchichak.

" 'Tis a fine conscience our friend has," exclaimed the ghost without a smile, nor did Radison ever see a smile on that stern-lipped mouth save once thereafter. "In with you, Uchichak! Do you fear divils before your God? In with you!"

And with one hand he not only flung the Crane head first into the chamber, but the shrinking chief lay quiet, fear in his eyes. Sulvent threw off his capote, and at the motion a crucifix slung on a moosehide thong slipped from his breast—the only sign yet which had denoted the man's order to Barr.

"No move from the enemy," he said as he crouched over the fire and ravenously seized a bit of the caribou steak. "Have you eaten? Good."

In fascinated silence the others watched him, Barr forgetting even the unknown horror that lay within the next chamber. Slowly Uchichak sat up with a feeble grasp at his lost dignity, and pulled out his pipe. When the last fragment of meat had been washed down with a slow drink from the pail, Sulvent turned abruptly to Barr, his hand out.

"You're Barr Radison? I'm Michael Sulvent, in charge of the Roman mission at Fort Tenacity—if so be there's any mission left! And this is Macklin, o' course—I've often heard Radison here speak of you."

"You've what?" exclaimed Barr, his fingers still tingling with the grip he received. "Why, I've never seen you before in my life, Père!"

"Sure not—well, I see there's nothin' for it but to talk, much as I hate the job. Do you keep quiet now, the both of you, and let's see if my afther-dinner speech will help to digest your tobacco."

The grim, ironic humor of the man was rendered all the grimmer for that the thin lips never curved in a smile. Montenay lay stretched out on the furs, stricken senseless.

"Just a minute, father," interposed Macklin. "Hadn't one of us better stand guard outside?"

"No need, Macklin. The divils are taking care of their dead, and we have an hour or two. To begin with, it was just sivin months ago to-day, when the winter darkness was falling, that Montenay gave me this, over the other side of the hills." He touched the scar on his brow.

"My skull was too thick for the bullet, by the kindness o' God, but he took me for dead and sent me over a cliff into the snow. 'Twas a kind bit, that, bein's it saved me from freezing, and when I came to I was snug and comfortable, barring a broken rib or two and the blood in my eye. As I lay there think-ing it over I saw 'twas a fine chance, so I thanked God for His mercies and went back to Murphy's."

Barr pictured that journey and shuddered.

"I got hold o' Jawn without Noreen or another soul seeing me, and Jawn—rest his soul—gave me dogs and food and a rifle. With them I turned back to these hills, and by the time the last dog was made into soup I was cured. One day I saw Montenay and followed him here."

"You know John Murphy is dead, then?" asked Barr.

"Now will you be keeping still and let a man talk? Of course he's dead—how else would Noreen be over yonder? Well, by little and little I discovered Montenay's secrets, knocking over a bird now and then for food, for you see he'd tried to shut God out o' his life and the lives of these Chipewas, which was wrong.

'Twas God looked afther me, for when he set out on his trip I was high starving; but the bones left in the village saved me for that time, afther they'd gone.

"Montenay didn't drink so hard then—I'm thinking he had to keep a stiff hand on the Chipewas after Nichemus came, for the breed made trouble. I was about ready to return to the fort with my information when he started on that trip. I waited to see what it was for, and when he came back with Noreen I was nigh forgetting that I'm a man of peace and that vengeance belongs with God. And so it does, look you! You're a wild divil, you American—well, you may be an instrument in a higher hand, anyhow.

"To come to the point, I've been in this cave many a time when Montenay was raving drunk, and many's the time I've talked with him, him thinking me a ghost. It was so I heard about you, Radison—faith, the man loved you like a brother and feared you like a divil at once!

"When you took Noreen away, I was watching from the hills. I saw the storm blowing up, so I made bold to guide you into the farther pass. I didn't dare to be joining you openly, for I had to keep an eye on Montenay's wildness, so when I saw Nichemus on your trail I tried to discourage him."

"It was you who stole his pail and shoes, then!" cried Barr, and glanced at the priest's tattered moccasins. "He's the one who made that track under the cliff, Mack! But go ahead, Père. Sorry I interrupted."

"You'd better be so. Afther Nichemus joined you and you were about to shoot him in your foolishness, I raised my voice and put the fear o' ghosts into him. Then you walked the valley beneath and raved at me, which was very impolitic. Don't be railing at the ghosts unless they do you harm, my son; if they aren't the right kind o' ghosts, it's like to be making them reverse their policy."

Macklin chuckled, and Radison felt himself redden slightly; but he nodded with a laugh, sure now that under his scarred, iron mask of a face this priest was a very human sort of a French-Irishman.

"Well, I never doubted that Nichemus would obey you, nor having had the secrets of his soul for a year past. So I set up one or two pointers overnight to guide you, as I had done before, if you remember, and what with hearing you talk and one thing or another I learned you expected Macklin.

"I left you to go home in peace, and returned to watch the proceedings here, which was foolish in me. Anyhow, you were recaptured, which I couldn't prevent; but when Montenay came here for that Bible he was soberer than I thought, and he had—"

"I know," laughed Radison with a glance at the still senseless giant. "He came back shaking like a leaf."

"That's the shank o' the story, my children—though, to tell the truth I'd hate to have a son who had no more sense than yourself, Barr Radison, for fear he'd be throwing me into the snow when I'd be afther birching him! Why, when the rifles blazed out and brought me down to save you to-night, I says to meself, 'Lord help us, Radison's on the rampage again!' And sure enough, he was. Now I misdoubt you've some questions to ask, so fire away while I have the time to waste on you."

Radison grinned happily, but it was Macklin who broke in with a question, while Uchichak sat over his pipe, eyes fastened on Père Sulvent with awe and admiration. The chief realized to the full all that lay behind that sketchy story of adventure and starvation in the Ghost Hills, and for once the bronze face was an open book to Barr.

"What are we going to do now, father?" asked the Canadian. "Here I'm laid up with two ribs and an ankle smashed, we have no food, Noreen's in the power of that devil Nichemus, and although the Sandfly is coming with the Crees, he may not be here for a week or more."

"My son, doubt yourself all you please, but don't be doubting Providence. It won't hurt you to chew these pelts for a while—I was six weeks, living on a dog a week, and afther that there were two weeks without dogs; but here I am, praise God.

"By good fortune I've a belt that I can draw tight, so while you're doing the fighting here I'll take a little trip through the gorge of darkness—regular valley of the shadow, it is—and it'll go hard, but I bring the Crees before you're too weak to pull trigger."

Suddenly Barr remembered the inner chamber, and realized that this was his chance to learn the secret of the Silent Ones, together with all the other things that had so puzzled him in the past few weeks. Knocking out his pipe, he extended the paper he had taken from Montenay.

"You probably know all about this, father. What's the meaning of it—what are the Silent Ones, and where did Montenay get that Bible you spoke of? There's a whole lot about this that I don't understand, and while I don't take any stock in this prophecy, as Montenay called it, I'm mighty interested in it on general principles. Is Montenay a trifle crazy, or what?"

" 'Tis said that we're all a bit touched in the head, according to the viewpoint, my son." Sulvent glanced at the paper and an expression of satisfaction swept over his virile face. "Ah, it's the last page of it—glory be, I've got it all!" With which he calmly folded the paper and shoved it into his ragged garments, then turned to Uchichak.

"Since you've seen all you'll be like to want of the other room, you might take a rifle and watch the mouth of the pass, as we've been talking overtime. And listen, my son! Those Silent Ones you saw are neither divils nor Spirit Dancers, but good sons of Mother Church, all three; what's more, I've given them my blessing, so now be off with you and have no fear."

Uchichak got into his capote and departed silently. Sulvent stared thoughtfully into the little fire for a moment, then his hard-set face came up.

"You've both read the paper? Well, 'tis a curious historical document, that, and I'm preserving the same, all of it, thanks be! Before I take you in there I'd better be telling you the story as I got it from the papers, so here goes."

The story that he told them there, with the firelight playing on his face and intensifying the domination and conscious mastery of each feature and line, was the tale of Pierre Radisson as set forth by the explorer's own hand—a lifelong habit which remained with him even to the end.

Cast off, betrayed by France and England alike in his old age, without share in the profits of that company of gentlemen adventurers trading into Hudson's Bay, which he had founded and fought for, Pierre Radisson had shaken off the spies who dogged him, and like the lion he was had returned to die in the wilderness he loved.

For comrades he had gathered a little band of aged Mohawks—men who had sworn brotherhood with him in the old days, and who, like all who ever followed him, were eager to seek death if it but won his smile and handclasp.

Traveling overland from York State with his war-wolves, fighters such as the frozen north had never seen before, they reached the bay, built canoes, and deliberately headed into the north beyond the outermost post of French or English.

Finding a Boston fur-pirate, Radisson calmly boarded her, set the men ashore, and proceeded with his Mohawk crew until the ice halted him and a storm drove his shattered craft on the coast.

In those days the Empty Places had indeed been empty, and after pushing into the Ghost Hills, Radisson knew that he faced his last trail. One by one hunger or scurvy seized the warriors; one by one they had died with a smile, until only a half-dozen reached the mouth of the terrible pass.

Radisson, Swift Arrow, and another called the Keeper of the Eastern Door of the Longhouse, an Iroquois title of dignify, remained in the cave while the others, being stronger, pushed on in search for game.

Such was the story as Père Sulvent had gathered it from the

papers scattered by Montenay and saved by him. Only the
prophecy had attracted the attention of the giant, and Sulvent
had been unable to get this last sheet until Barr handed it to
him.

"Well, what next?" inquired Macklin excitedly. Sulvent
looked square at him.

"There was no next. Radisson and the Mohawks are still
waiting, that's all."

"Then that's where Montenay got the wampum belt and the
flintlock pistol," began Barr eagerly; but he broke off to stare
suddenly at Sulvent. "Say, do you mean that they are alive? I
thought Montenay was lying about—"

"Père Sulvent! Père Sulvent!"

The agonized wail that burst from Montenay was pitiful and
brought all three men about instantly. The giant, ghastly of face,
was staring at Sulvent with bulging eyes; but there was no re-
laxation of the priest's iron face when he spoke.

"Macferris Montenay, you denied your God when He had
favored you, and with murder in your heart you blasphemed
and shot down God's minister. You've been in my hands a
hundred times within the last month, and now the time has
come—for vengeance is the right of God alone. Repent! Faith,
'tis the last chance you'll have, my son, for you've many murders
on your soul, from Jawn Murphy to—"

"Ye hound of hell!" Radison leaped to his feet as a wild roar
burst from the giant and he tore at his bonds, his mouth
foaming. "So you're man and no ghost! I'll rip the heart out of
ye yet, ye—"

He fell to cursing at the top of his voice; but Père Sulvent
leaned over, carefully selected a magnificent black-fox skin, and
with his ironic, mirthless humor dropped it over the distorted
face of Montenay.

"As man to man, Montenay, I forgive you readily; as priest
to man I'd forgive you if you'd repent; but as Irishman to
Scotchman—I wish to hell I had ye in my naked hands, wid

God to be judgin' us, an'tis little need of forgiveness ye'd have, ye scut!"

For a bare instant a wave of ferocity swept into that terrible scarred face, then it passed instantly, and Sulvent rose.

"Come, my sons—we'll be paying a bit of a visit to Pierre Radisson, yonder."

CHAPTER XVI

THE SILENT ONES

"UP ON that ledge of rock there's a candle, Radison," said Père Sulvent. "Better use it."

Barr saw an out-jutting ledge near the opening, felt for the candle, and found it. As he lit it at the fire he saw Sulvent bend over and pick up Macklin as if he were a babe, and he realized what mighty strength there must be in that tall frame.

"Does it hurt you, so?" asked the priest, and Macklin shook his head, his eyes alight with eagerness. At a nod from Sulvent, Barr raised the candle and stepped through the opening with a little shiver that changed to a startled cry as he saw what lay ahead.

For there, staring at him from one side of a rude-table, knife upraised to strike, was an Indian such as he had never seen except in pictures—with wrinkled, paint-splashed face, head shaven save for a gray scalplock, dangling eagle feather over one ear, and fearful, widely open eyes staring straight into his!

Small wonder that the Crane had fled before that terrible scene, for as Radison caught a gasp from Macklin behind, he raised the candle with shaking fingers, and disclosed two more figures.

"Jumping Sandhills!" came the hoarse exclamation from Macklin. "Are they alive? As I live, Barr, look at yourself!"

Radison felt a thrill of unspeakable horror as he gazed, and set the candle on the table with nerveless hand. Looking squarely at him was a face that might have been his own but for its age and the white hair around it, and the thing unnerved him. There was the same high brow and deep-set, far-searching eyes; the same nose and mouth and chin; the same general appearance of a brooding eagle seeking where to strike. In the hand was a quill pen, and the rough table was littered with objects.

Barr wiped the sweat from his face, trembling, a mad impulse hot upon him to turn and fly from the place before those terrible figures spoke. During that first minute he did not doubt that they were alive. Suddenly the ringing voice of Sulvent filled the room.

"Up with the candle, Barr—high above your head!"

He obeyed mechanically, and looking at the naked Mohawk before him, uttered a low, hysterical laugh as he realized everything in a flash. From the waist down the figure was of solid, translucent rock, while the glisten and glitter of the portion above the table, and the steady dripping of water, frozen as it fell, told the story.

The third figure—another but smaller and more wrinkled Indian—was crouched behind the table in an attitude of hopeless waiting, and only his head and shoulders were incased in the rock-drippings from above.

"Cold-storage it is," echoed the reassuring tones of Sulvent. "From one thing and another, too long to be explaining here, I figure that they closed the place against the cold at first, so that the dripping from above ran on down and formed stalagmites like those scattered around yonder. Then the cold got in and froze them over, so keeping them safe and sound till judgement day."

Barr glanced around and saw long stalactites depending from the high roof in innumerable clusters, thousands of them, while others filled the floor of the cave. On the table were one or two odd knives, a broken flintlock pistol, powder-horns, paint-bags, and other articles. With a sigh of relief Radison turned, at Sulvent's order.

"It's weary I'm getting, Macklin, so let's go back unless you'd like to move your bed in here. Also, it's just occurred to me that I've been doing all the talking and don't know yet how you got hurt, though you said your leg was broke."

When they were once more in the outer chamber, where Montenay lay in seeming quiet, Sulvent gleaned what scraps he needed to piece out their stories, while he unwrapped Macklin's leg and side with tender hands. The dressings and splints of Uchichak's making had been rude but serviceable, and he nodded complacently.

"Healing fine—we'll do no better than to put these on again, Barr."

Radison could not get the thought of those three figures out of his head. Now he knew why Montenay had termed them, in brutal jest, the Silent Ones; now he understood the mortal anguish of Nichemus at the giant's threat to leave him with Radisson, and the superstitious grip which Montenay held on the Chipewas.

"He used to bring the chiefs here and scare 'em," commented Sulvent. "I take it that the inner cave was blocked up, and that he found it one day while he was knocking around. Anyhow, I've got a plan. If I can locate the Crees down the gorge, I'll bring them around—"

What that plan was Père Sulvent never explained. Radison caught something that sounded like a bestial snarl, the fire was scattered far and wide over the pelts amid a shower of sparks, and as he glimpsed a huge form that locked with the priest and bore him backward he realized what must have happened.

While they had been in the other chamber Montenay had loosened his bonds—perhaps by his giant strength, perhaps by means of the fire—and had chosen his time to spring on Sulvent. There was work to be done, however, and at Macklin's cry Barr awoke.

Stamping out the sparks that were fast filling the cave with the pungent odor of burning hair and hide, he managed to collect a few brands in frenzied haste. They blazed up fitfully, and leaping to the side of Macklin, to protect him from the two fighting men, Barr seized the revolver that the other held out.

He could not use it, however. As the tiny fire-blaze shot up he saw the two great bodies locked tightly together; both men were on their feet, swaying and rocking and reeling to and fro, while the small chamber was filled with hoarse panting and the thud of blows. Radison groaned as he watched the dark forms, then the flicker of light blazed out clear and bright, and he uttered a gasp of astonishment.

For Père Sulvent, his scarred face set in terrible lines of rage, had forced Montenay against the wall, disregarding the great hands that clutched and tore at his throat, and with deliberate ferocity was driving his fist into the bearded face. Radison saw the blood leap after each blow, saw Sulvent suddenly tear back from Montenay's grip—and the priest caught the giant and swung him full over his hip, to fall with a crash against the opposite wall.

Before the horrified Radison could fire the two men were locked again. But this time the struggle was short. As Montenay lurched up Sulvent was ready; he gripped the other man in those iron hands, twisted him about suddenly, and struck him twice in the body, instantly leaping away.

Two blows—no more; but Barr had distinctly heard two dull crunches, sickening him, for he knew well what it portended. Montenay stood erect a moment, then his head flung back and he went over in a heap, while Sulvent gravely examined his knuckles.

" 'Tis a sinful man I am," he said, regaining his calm after one deep breath. "I have not used those murderin' blows since the day I left the regiment—God save us, but I bruk me hand on him! One took his collarbone and the other his ribs, and I'm thinking there'll be no need of tying him up more."

Taking a step forward, Barr knelt and Sulvent joined him. The bearded face was a mask of blood, and as he felt beneath the buckskin shirt Radison's face grew white. The giant's collarbone was smashed and the ribs of his left side seemed as though driven in by a trip-hammer, great gasping breaths coming from the red-foamed mouth.

"No, he's not dead," said Sulvent grimly. Barr staggered to his feet, sick and faint, while Macklin stared with blazing eyes from a bloodless face. "Ye'll be needing a breath of air, Radison—take a rifle and look up the Crane, if you like, while I'm doing what can be done for this poor divil. God forgive me, but the strength jumps into me when I'm near him!"

Radison answered no word, but seized his capote and rifle and staggered for the open air. He could fight if necessary, and fight with his whole soul, but such battle as this had been was more than fighting. It was the meeting of Titans, in a red-lusting, primal hand-grip that knew only one ending. He did not blame Sulvent, but the tremendously powerful face of the man was borne out in those two murderous blows, and the short struggle had sickened him.

"Cave men!" he thought to himself as he drew a deep breath of cold air at the entrance of the cave. "Fighting as their ancestors fought thousands of years ago. Well, Montenay has met his match, at least! He had it coming to him, and he forced the issue; so there's no more to be said, I suppose. Now to find Uchichak."

Slipping into Sulvent's shoes in place of his own, he uncased his rifle, saw that it was loaded, and started for the entrance of the gorge. Here he stood motionless, seeing no sign of the chief, and watched the scene before him.

On the left of the cañon's mouth, where that inner passage stretched away dark and menacing in the dull afternoon sunlight, a single figure stood atop the fallen rocks four hundred yards away. Radison guessed that he was a sentinel and looked about for the camp. This lay out in the shelter of one of the bare rock ridges and directly opposite the mouth of the gorge.

A few fires had been built, and around these were gathered some thirty or forty figures, whose number Barr could only guess at roughly. Below lay the village, and among the lodges squaws and boys were moving. On the whole, Radison was surprised at the apathy which seemed to have fallen upon the Chipewas; for Jean Nichemus was no man to remain quiet once he knew where his foe lay.

"I'll bet that appearance of Sulvent's scared Jean pretty stiff," mused the American, reflecting on the events of the night before. "Still, they wouldn't guess that we know anything about the Silent Ones, and probably dope it out that we're simply holding the gorge; but if they're waiting for Crazy Bear to break out and join them they'll have a mighty long wait! Wonder where the Crane is?"

Turning, he searched the outer fragments of shattered rock at the base of the cliffs, but could see nothing of Uchichak. A keen scrutiny of each side of the entrance itself, which was hardly more than a dozen feet across, failed to reveal anything. Above, the crags towered apart as if a wedge-shaped section had been sliced out of the line of cliffs.

As Barr looked up he was suddenly aware of a dark, grinning face just above his head on the opposite side of the notch. With an exclamation of belief he started across, for the Crane was comfortably ensconced on a ledge, fortified with a few rocks, from which the approach to the gorge could be swept with ease.

"Strong Eyes get weak, huh?" he grunted amiably as he helped Barr to clamber up.

"I wasn't looking for you on the cliff," laughed the American. "This is a pretty slick little fortification, chief! What's doing with the Chipewas?"

"The Crane has eyes, but they cannot read hearts, Strong

Eyes. They have seen me, but they have not fired, nor have I. My brother is very cunning—perhaps he can tell who that is?"

As he spoke the Crane pointed to the village. Barr followed the gesture and saw a figure standing in the door of a shack. It was too far away to make out the face, but a glint of gold flashed in the sun, and his heart leaped.

"Noreen! Minebegonequay!"

Uchichak smiled to himself, and a moment later the figure vanished within the shack.

Radison tried to catch sight of Nichemus, but the breed was not visible, and he told Uchichak of the fight in the cave. The chief heard him with unconcealed satisfaction.

"Miwasin! Now Crazy Bear will die, and my young men will sweep over the Chipewas very easily—"

"I'd much prefer to be alive when they do it," broke in Barr dryly. "As it is, we may have to stay here for a week without food. Isn't there some way we could get Minebegonequay out of that village, chief?"

Without hesitation Uchichak shook his head.

"No. Ask Père Sulvent."

There being no prospect of anything stirring, Barr left the Cree philosophically smoking his pipe and made his way back to the cavern, not without a shrinking dread of what he might find there. He was determined to get Noreen away from Nichemus if that was possible, and imagined that by playing ghost again Sulvent might turn the trick.

He found the "man of peace" just finishing his work of bandaging Montenay, who still lay breathing stertorously, unconscious. Macklin was fretting at his own impotence, and when Barr had explained what he wanted the Canadian urged Sulvent to at least attempt getting Noreen away. The priest listened impassively.

"No. My sons, Noreen is in no danger, I take it. Nichemus wants her as his wife, and he'll not touch her until the church marries him. That's his nature, for he's superstitious to the marrow. On the other hand, you'll be finding yourselves in a tight hole before long, I'm thinking. He'll be cooking up some diviltry, never fear, and the sooner I get away to bring the Crees the better it'll be for us all."

"I suppose you're right, father," admitted the American slowly, perceiving the force of the argument. "When do you think you'd better start? Is there anything we can do to help her?"

"Nothing. As for starting, I'll be on my way in five minutes. Now, mind, you'll have to stand a siege, for these Chipewas won't be scared of the Silent Ones when it comes to paying for blood with blood. You'd better store up some snow in the passage, where it'll keep frozen; afther it gives out you can melt ice from the other room, where there's like to be enough to last you until I return. Don't let the divils bring up wood, mind, or you'll be smoked out in no time."

With this advice Père Sulvent discarded his tattered capote and took the bearskin which Montenay had worn. There was a good store of wood for the fire, and he took what matches the two men had, as Uchichak's fire-bag could be fallen back on in case of need. Then, handing Barr the cartridges he had left, he held out one hand with a last touch of his unsmiling, ironic, yet deeply earnest nature.

"*Pax vobiscum*, my sons—though it's little pax you're likely to have afther I go. At all events, you're in the right, so take my blessing and my cartridges together, and see you use 'em both well. Whatcheer!"

"Whatcheer! Whatcheer!" repeated Macklin and Radison together, and the priest was gone.

So impressed had they been with the powerful nature of the man that with his departure a loneliness seemed to settle on the cavern, as if their greatest support had been withdrawn. Barr shook off this feeling with an effort, drew out his pipe, and when the two men were smoking together the sense of loneliness gradually disappeared.

"Hope he pulls through!" exclaimed Macklin. "What a face

he has! Hear his little remark about the regiment, Barr? That man would take a chance on storming hell itself!"

The American nodded.

"Great character, Mack. Say, do you remember the day after we'd left Tenacity, when Nichemus had shot one of the dogs?"

"You mean our little talk? Sure I do." The Canadian grinned quickly. "Why? Found out I was right, have you?"

"Uh-huh. I'm done, old man. If we ever get out of this mess I guess home and fireside will do for me in future. I'm kind of glad I'm not nineteen, after all."

Macklin puffed silently for a moment, dryly eying the American.

"I'd like to have an introduction," he spoke as if to himself, "but I suppose this darned big-nosed devil wants to hog everything—"

With a great laugh Radison held out his hand.

"Shake, Tom! You'll be best man, and Père Sulvent—"

The words were stopped by a tremendous roaring crash from outside, the rolling echoes filling the cave with thunderous waves of sound. Catching at his rifle, Radison leaped to his feet and dashed for the entrance.

CHAPTER XVII

BESIEGED

BEFORE HE gained the front of the winding passage there came another roaring crash of sound, and, with anxiety tearing at his heart, Barr rushed out into the dim light of the narrow gorge. As he reached the mouth of the cavern a dark figure scrambled up the broken rocks, and Uchichak gained the shelter of the rift.

Barely was the Cree panting at his side when, as Barr looked up, he saw something leaping from side to side of the rock walls, rending and splitting fragments of the granite, and a second later a tremendous boulder plunged down against a jutting point of the wall, split with a roar, and sent rock splinters flying.

"Dat dam' Nichemus!" sputtered the angry Uchichak. "Send de men on cliffs, t'row rock down—miss me so much!"

He held his hands six inches apart, and Radison did not need to question him to see that the escape must have been a close one, for a jagged splinter had been ripped from the stock of the chief's rifle. Then began a new and extremely exciting sport— if sport it could be called—for the American.

This consisted in looking up at the towering crags and watching those boulders come slithering down, leaping and rocking from side to side, bringing a whole avalanche in their train, until they either shot into the deep snow or burst on some projection.

At first he tried to catch sight of some figure above, and even sent a futile bullet rattling up the cliff; but no one could be seen, and the tremendous fascination of watching those boulders plunge down at about one-minute intervals gripped him intensely, though more than once fragments were sent crashing into the cave mouth.

At all events, Nichemus had accomplished his purpose of clearing out the mouth of the gorge, for the wedge-shaped notch offered no protection to Uchichak's ledge, and it would be madness to have remained there. The narrow, snow-covered floor of the cañon was strewn with half-buried boulders and rock splinters, and after ten minutes Radison perceived that the bombardment had ceased. He was standing gazing up when Uchichak dragged him inside with an angry exclamation, and something spattered viciously on the rock behind.

Awaking to the danger and flinging off the fascination which had gripped him, Barr flung up his rifle and sent a bullet at one or two figures near the entrance of the gorge. The Crane followed suit, and the Chipewas vanished; but they had gained the desired lodgment among the rocks, and now the cañon rolled with the echoes of shots, while bullets flattered and bit at the mouth of the cavern.

Too late Radison recalled Sulvent's warning about the snow, for now it was impossible to collect any with the bullets from the entrance sweeping down the narrow cleft. Their only resource would be the frozen drippings in the chamber of the dead—a thought that did not particularly appeal to the American.

However, with the ceasing of the bombardment from above, Uchichak sprang into action. Risking the bullets that plowed past, he reached out after one or two fragments of rock, and these, with what already lay inside the cave entrance, made a very passable barrier. Lying down behind this, the two men began a slow, methodical effort to keep the enemy in check, in which Barr shaded the Indian's dislike of wasting a single cartridge.

"If we only had something to work with," he said to the Crane, "we could plant one of these kegs of powder out there. However, it might be no good after two hundred years of inaction, and we have nothing of which to lay a train—except the stuff itself. Did the Père get off all right?"

Uchichak nodded, but wasted no words in speaking, and Barr gave up the idea of using Pierre Radisson's old stock of powder. Now he gave himself to the work in hand, and after he had picked off one dark figure which he detected climbing along a ledge of the opposite wall the eagerness of the Chipewas was considerably dampened.

"If you'll hold them," he said to the chief, after a couple of hours, "I'll melt up some ice. We'll have to keep that tea-pail going—whew! I don't fancy a week of this sort of thing!"

Uchichak nodded, and, leaving his rifle for use in case of a sudden rush— which was very improbable—Barr returned to the inner chamber. He found Montenay as he had been left, but Barr made no effort to revive him.

"We'd do him no good, Tom," he said in reply to the Canadian's protest. "He's not suffering now, anyway, and he'd only be an added bother if he were awake. Don't fear, we'll have to look after him soon enough!"

While he worked at his highly distasteful task of chopping out chunks of ice from the next room, Barr kept up a rattling conversation with Macklin. The more he saw of the Silent Ones the less he blamed Nichemus or any one else for their superstition. In the flickering candle-light those frozen figures seemed ready to break out into speech at any moment, but as Barr conquered his unreasoning fear he saw that Père Sulvent had told the true story. All three faces were hollow of cheek, while the huddled-up Mohawk still held a strip of mooseskin he had been gnawing when he died.

No doubt Radisson had seized those black-and-silver fox skins from the fur pirates, or perhaps had traded them as he journeyed from the coast. In any case, the mystery which had brought Macklin here was solved, thought Barr. No more pelts would ever go out from John Murphy, the free-trader, and he grimly congratulated the Canadian on the success of his mission, while the occasional reports of Uchichak's rifle filled the cave with echo.

"Hey!" Macklin stopped him as he was returning for more ice, "why not take out a keg of powder and let her off in the gorge?"

"I thought of that," and Barr grinned. "Do you know any way of getting it out and laying a train without being bowled over by a Chipewa? Besides, if we let off a blast out there it might be blamed unhealthy for any one inside here; these cliffs seem to be rotten with ice-drip, and I'd hate to risk it."

"Shucks! I'd take a chance on it, Rad. I tell you—if you get a chance just dump out a keg and lay a train loose. Then if they make a charge you could set it off. Go ahead and do it. I'll 'tend to the kettle."

So Barr drew the eager Canadian closer to the fire, where he could reach the pail at ease, and carried out a couple of the powder-kegs. He explained his purpose to Uchichak, and it was decided that at the first opportunity the rock ascent leading to the cave should be well heaped with loose powder, while a trail could be laid on pelts placed end to end.

The slow hours passed without change, one or two bullets singing past the cave-mouth at intervals, and not until the night had nearly gone did Barr dare to venture forth, the opened kegs under his arms. He dumped the contents in a loose pile, while Uchichak made ready the skins, a third keg providing a generous train back to the cave-mouth. Then the hides were securely weighted down with rocks, and the two returned.

A few bullets had gone over them, but the Chipewa muskets were poor weapons at a hundred yards of semi-darkness, and Barr heard nothing of Nichemus and the rifle, for which he was profoundly grateful.

Now began a weary, heart-breaking drag of a time that seemed like a nightmare to Radison whenever he looked back on it. The expected attack did not materialize, but the Chipewas at the mouth of the pass kept sending an occasional shot to show that they were on the alert, and for the two men in the cavern the slow hours seemed like days.

Barr finally returned to the chamber and flung himself down to sleep, and when day had come upon the land outside that valley of shadow Uchichak roused him and sent him out to stand guard.

All that morning Radison lay behind the barricade of rocks, uncertain whether his shots were taking effect, for not once did he catch sight of a moving figure. Evidently Nichemus was satisfied that he had egress from the cave blocked, for no more boulders crashed down, and Radison speculated vainly as to what was brewing.

The Chipewas would have little stomach for a direct attack; but Nichemus was cunning of brain, and was more to be feared than Montenay had the giant led his men.

When Uchichak once more relieved him, long after midday,

Barr returned to find Montenay conscious. Macklin had been bathing the shattered face of the giant with some of their precious water, but at sight of the wrecked man Radison had no heart to protest.

He sat down beside Montenay and took the feeble hand that was extended to him, a great surge of pity rising in his soul, for this was the most pitiful of all sights—a broken body whose stern will rose superior to the ills of the flesh.

"Well, ye win, Radisson!" Montenay tried to smile, but without success. "I've done a sight o' wrong, and—and Père Sulvent had more behind him than I had." For an instant there was a flicker of the old, eager wistfulness in voice and eyes. "I don't blame ye, Radisson, for ye loved Noreen, too—but, oh, man! Had ye but joined with me we would ha' done such things!"

"I'm sorry, Montenay; but you couldn't have expected me to join you if you'd used your brains a bit. You should have seen that. However, it's all past and done now, old man; and we're up against it together. Do you think that Nichemus would obey you?"

"He swore on the crucifix!" gasped Montenay. "Talking Owl would obey me if the breed wouldn't. I'm not a dead man yet, Radisson."

"I hope not—" began the American, when a shrill yell from Uchichak brought him to his feet, and he ran for the entrance.

He was surprised to see Uchichak standing, rifle in hand, as if rooted to the spot. When he gained sight of the floor of the gorge he gave an exclamation. There, moving in from the mouth of the opening, was a solid black mass from which spat fire, while the bullets sung around and past the cave entrance. For a second Radison stared in consternation, then realization flashed over him as the thing came to within fifty yards.

"By thunder—Birnam Wood come to Dunsinane!" The wild cry burst from his lips as his rifle went up. "Nichemus has made screens—shoot, chief! Shoot at the feet!"

The Crane did not understand, but he obeyed promptly.

Despite the bullets, that black mass, formed of saplings lashed together and borne by Chipewas, forged ahead steadily, swiftly, leaving one or two bodies behind.

A wild yell of hatred and exultation pealed up, for the narrow gorge allowed a large party to get behind the screens without fear of an enfilading fire, and Radison knew that before he could reload his magazine the Chipewas would be on them. Then, with the wall of saplings rushing toward him a scant twenty yards away, he drew out Macklin's revolver with a shout:

"Reload the rifles—quick! Get back inside and shoot!"

Barr put the automatic across the pelt that held the train of powder and waited. The muskets had ceased spitting fire, for those at the mouth of the gorge could not shoot now for fear of hitting the men crowded behind the screen of saplings. Radison's hand trembled on the trigger; but he waited grimly, staking all on this one cast.

If the powder was bad, if the stuff failed to go off, he and Uchichak would be gone before they could even start to fight. Besides, he must wait until the Chipewas were almost upon the powder, if it was to take effect.

Forward they dashed, while the Crane frantically reloaded the two magazines. At ten yards Radison's nerve almost failed him, but he repressed the impulse to shoot and waited until that tall wooden mass was a bare ten feet from the cave. Already it was giving way, shaking and quivering as the eager Chipewas perceived their success, and it threatened to disintegrate at any second into a mass of men. Radison dared wait no longer; making sure that the automatic was touching the powder, he pulled the trigger and sent a single shot over the pelt into that wooden wall, leaping back as he did so.

Only the leap saved him, for he had forgotten that the extremely narrow gorge, acting even on loose powder, would serve to compress the explosion and lend it terrific force. As his revolver spoke there came a tiny flash of red from the train; then a deep-toned, sullen roar, and up into the cañon shot a spreading burst of flame, followed by a flood of choking smoke that rolled in great clouds over everything.

Barr was flung back bodily against Uchichak, and as the two men went to the floor the American had a glimpse of a swarm of horror-struck faces and scattering men, while the shield of saplings had been riven asunder by the blast. Then the smoke covered him, and he lay close to the cavern floor, gasping for breath.

During one moment there was dread silence without, until the storm of wild shrieks that burst forth was drowned in a roar and rattle of rock, and with a shudder Radison guessed that the shock had brought down loose overhangs from the cliff—with a result that he hardly dared picture to himself.

Slowly the rending echoes died away down the towering crags, and with a choking cough Radison put out his hands, feeling. He touched the body of Uchichak, and, as the chief lay inert beneath his grip, Barr rose swiftly and dragged the Crane through the passage by one shoulder, sudden fear coming over him that Uchichak had been killed.

Stumbling into the rock-chamber, he found that, although the smoke was eddying in thickly, it was caught and whirled into the inner room by the draft, and knew that there were openings through the roof. Disregarding Macklin's cry, he turned to Uchichak, and as he did so the chief opened his eyes.

"Huh! Dam' plenty smoke!"

The American sank down with a burst of hysterical laughter, realizing that the Crane had merely had the wind knocked out of him. Macklin's hand gripped him and restored him to himself on the instant.

"What happened, Barr—the powder?"

Radison nodded, and his face suddenly grew white as he thought of the Chipewas who had been caught in that deluge of flame and shattered rock. With a cry to Uchichak, he gained his feet and strode out of the chamber, and the chief followed closely on his heels.

It was not in the heart of the American to let any man, friend or foe, suffer, as there must be men suffering out in that gorge; and it never entered his head that Uchichak might misunderstand his motive, nor did he catch the glint of steel that came from the other's hand when they stepped out into the smoke-hung entrance.

The narrow gorge was almost clear of the fumes, however, for the tearing wind that eternally ripped down through the chasm had driven the smoke before it, and all things lay plain in the dim light that filtered down.

Splintered saplings lay strewn like matches among the rocks, and as Barr hastily clambered down the incline from the cave he heard a faint groan and detected two or three bodies, which writhed aimlessly.

Horror in his eyes, the American yet felt a thrill of relief that it was no worse, and rushed to pull up the nearest Chipewa. Finding the blackened man alive and but pinned down by a block of stone, he extricated him and handed him over to Uchichak, hastening on to the next.

This, to his surprise, proved to be no other than Talking Owl, who gravely held forth a hand at his approach; and Radison drew him from beneath a fragment of the sapling shield. The Chipewa chief had been protected by this from the fall of rock, though he was terribly bruised. Just as he ascertained this, Barr suddenly saw a ferocious look leap into the man's face, and with a quick movement knocked the gleaming knife from the other's hand angry at the treachery.

"Haven't you any decency—"!

The American stopped and whirled about, for Talking Owl's features were convulsed with rage; but his eyes were fixed on an object behind Barr. To the latter's dismay, he saw the Crane coolly wiping his knife on the body of the man first saved!

"You fiend!" shouted Barr furiously. "What do you mean by that?"

Uchichak, startled, looked up. An expression of surprise flitted over his dark face.

"Huh? Would my brother let these Chipewa dogs live?"

"That's what I came out for," snapped Barr, remembering that Uchichak's code of ethics was not his own. "Did you murder him?"

For answer the chief stared at him a moment in disgust, then turned and without a word vanished into the cave entrance. Striding to the prostrate body, Radison found the man stabbed to the heart.

"Help me with the rest, Talking Owl," he said simply, realizing now what that quick knife-flash had meant.

"You be good warrior, Strong Eyes," said the Chipewa, patting Barr on the shoulder. "No kill you, no kill company man, huh? Kill Uchichak—gurr-r-r!"

They found two more living Chipewas, whom Radison despatched to their own people, much to their astonishment. Besides these, three had been killed by the explosion, and how many had been wounded Barr had no means of knowing. When he was sure that there were no others, he took Talking Owl's arm and motioned toward the cavern. The chief hesitated, his deep eyes searching the American's face.

"Talking Owl no like de Silent Ones."

"You won't see them," smiled Radison. "Montenay is there—the king, you know. Come along—don't hang back like a frightened squaw, Talking Owl!"

Bowing his head as if ready for what might befall, the Chipewa strode up into the cavern, seeming to know the way perfectly, and Barr had no doubt that Montenay had fetched him there before on less pleasant errands.

When they reached the cave, where Uchichak was sullenly smoking, Radison explained everything to Macklin and Montenay. The latter addressed Talking Owl in Chipewa, and after a moment spoke in English.

"Nichemus is in command, of course, and Talking Owl

doesn't like it. They've been hanging off, expecting me back, and the chief has a proposition. He has nothing special against Macklin, and offers you, Radisson, peace in exchange for me. The Crane dies."

"And Noreen," softly asked Barr. "You give her up, Montenay?"

"When I'm dead—not before!" Faintly the indomitable will-power of the man flamed out.

"All right." The American turned to the Chipewa. "Promise to send us meat and you go free. Montenay—the king, here—stays. Will you send food at once?"

Talking Owl nodded slowly.

"Very well—go."

CHAPTER XVIII

NICHEMUS PLAYS TRUMP

"FUNNY HOW folks jump at things, Barr. Uchichak saw those fellows in there and took 'em for the Spirit Dancers. The Chipewas were satisfied to call 'em the Silent Ones and let it go at that. He comes along"—and Macklin nodded at the sleeping form of Montenay—"and gets the fool notion that the verse out on the wall is his luck, and that Pierre had donated the Ghost Hills as a kingdom to whoever found him. Queer, eh?"

"Human nature, Tom—and I don't blame Montenay for being half crazy. Between the liquor, these black-fox pelts, and association with the three dead men yonder, any man would have license to go off his head. If Sulvent doesn't bring the Crees pretty soon—well, I guess I'll give Uchichak a bit of sleep."

Macklin put out a detaining hand.

"Leave me that automatic, Rad," he said quietly. "The chief's been acting like a husky dog. He'll sit over there and never sleep a wink, but just glower at Montenay and finger his knife. It looks pretty bad. Thanks. See you later!"

Two nights had passed since the attack—two weary nights and a day. Talking Owl had sent a generous supply of caribou meat and flour, and not a shot had been fired; but the cavern was well watched and the tension had been hard on the spirits of all except Montenay, whose enforced abstinent from liquor seemed a good thing for him. He was able to crawl about the chamber, on oath not to attempt escape, for Barr believed that the oath would be kept.

After relieving the sullen Cree, Barr, haggard and weary, stretched out on some furs and lit his pipe, idly watching the smoke drift out and up. Suddenly he was startled by a hail, and jumped up to see the figure of Nichemus approaching from the mouth of the gorge, ostentatiously waving a branch. Radison held up empty hands, and the breed came on confidently.

"*B'jou, b'jou!*" he grinned as he came to the cavern. "You's be grow de beard, eh?"

Involuntarily Radison passed his hand over his stubby chin and laughed.

"What are you after, Nichemus? Want to patch up a truce?"

"Mebbe." Sobered, Nichemus flung a swift glance behind him. "Dat fellair Talking Owl, she's be de debil for make trouble, *msieu!* She's say get Mont'ney, den we make for fight. She's say de king he's ver' sick. I t'ink he's be de big liar, eh?"

Radison nodded down into the curious, searching eyes.

"It's so, Jean. Montenay's pretty badly off. So the Chipewas won't fight till you get Montenay? You'll be a long time without a scrap, I'm afraid!"

Nichemus grinned confidently, coolly joined Barr on the ledge, and filled his pipe as he squatted down comfortably.

"Now, *m'sieu,* listen." The breed spoke earnestly, his roving eyes flitting about, and Barr guessed that his superstitious fear of the place had not vanished. "De Chip'was lak for keel de

Crane, *oui*. Den dey say I's be no good. *M'sieu*, I t'ink me dey make for keel me yet!"

Radison was not greatly impressed by Jean's manner.

"How is Minebegonequay?" he asked. The breed's dark features lit up for an instant.

"I'm come to dat. Lissen! S'pose me I take de sled wit de grub, make for steal Minebegonequay, run lak hell for here—you make for help, *m'sieu?*"

Radison stared, astounded, but the other met his gaze squarely. This was the last thing the American looked for—that Nichemus should deliberately offer to get Noreen out of the village and to the cave, with food. What could be back of it?

"See here, Jean," he said sternly, "you're either lying or else you've reformed a whole lot of late. You know that you'll never marry Noreen while I live, so why should you bring her to me? Don't try any crooked tricks or you're apt to see Père Sulvent again!"

The brown features shot white at the name, and fear leaped into the dark eyes; but Nichemus quickly pulled himself together.

"Lissen! I make for see Minebegonequay—she's not spik to me, she's be ver' proud, ver' col'. She's be hurt me here," and he tapped his breast, "an' I t'ink me dem Chip'was make for keel me pretty soon. *M'sieu*, I love her, *oui*, but I'm be 'fraid for stay on dat village. So I's bring her here, make for help you, fight lak hell for lick dem Chip'was. *Non?* Den mebbe we's have de gran' scrap, you an' me, *m'sieu!*"

"Well, you're certainly frank about it!" exclaimed the astonished American. "So you figure out that it's better to combine with me against the Chipewas, and after they're licked you can chance it with me, eh?"

Nichemus nodded eagerly, his white teeth flashing out, and Barr thought it over. He did not doubt that Nichemus, through his unsuccessful leadership, might have lost favor with the Chipewas; but that they would kill him was rather improbable, even in revenge for the loss of their warriors. However, the breed seemed to have that idea firmly implanted in his mind, and Radison was forced to the conclusion that the offer was made in good faith. The accession of another rifle and a sled of provisions would practically mean that the cave could be held until the Crees arrived.

Radison chuckled to himself at the thought, for Nichemus was evidently in blissful ignorance of the fact that the Crees were coming. Their arrival would simplify matters as regarded Nichemus, he reflected, for the breed would then be helpless.

"I'll go you, Nichemus," he said slowly. "What do you want me to do?"

"Make de lettair," replied the other swiftly, his eyes gleaming. "Say to Minebegonequay for come wit' me. She's no spik to me, *m'sieu*, but mebbe she come for you, eh?"

Barr caught that sudden gleam in the dark eyes and frowned. He realized, however, that if Noreen shut herself off from Nichemus, as was probably the case, only a letter from him could get her to trust the breed.

"Wait here," he said and entered the rock-chamber. Macklin alone was awake, and without a word to him Barr took a small silver-fox skin and with a charred stick from the fire wrote his brief message on the brown underside of the pelt.

NOREEN: Jean brings you to me.
BARR.

Slipping out to the entrance again, he took off his mitten, pulled a battered seal-ring from his finger, and handed it with the skin to Nichemus.

"She will recognize that ring. When will you come?"

"I t'ink me to-morrow mornin', early! You make for watch?"

Radison nodded, and as Nichemus walked away, he felt vaguely uneasy. Then he shook the feeling off and re-entered the cavern, finding Montenay awake.

"Was that Nichemus I heard talkin'?" asked the giant quietly.

Without hesitation the American related his conversation, Uchichak waking and listening with the rest. When Barr was through the chief gave a disgusted sniff and stalked forth to guard-mount, though it was not yet time for that, and for a little there was silence.

Montenay sat stiffly, a mass of sticking-plaster and bandages, from which swept shreds of his great beard, while his eyes flamed dully into the fire. Macklin toyed idly with a paint-bag Barr had brought him from that fearsome table in the other chamber, while Radison himself stretched out on the pelts and dozed, willing to let Uchichak play sentry if he liked.

"An' ye told him I was knocked out—oh, ye utter fool!"

The slow, scornful words pierced through Radison's doze and bit into his brain. He sat up, staring, and found Montenay's eyes on him.

"Huh? What was that?"

Montenay did not answer at once. The Canadian ceased to play with the buckskin bag and frowned suddenly.

"You took a chance on trusting a breed—and it's a darned long chance, believe me! No wonder it made the chief sore."

In blank consternation the American looked from one to the other. Montenay spoke up again, with a painful wag of his great head as if thinking aloud.

"Aye, Nichemus has been a thorn in my side since he drifted up, two years an' more ago. I scared him—or I thought I did; by Jasper, that's a queer yarn he dished up! I wonder, now—I wonder! Man, but it don't sound right!"

"Nonsense," said Barr with an uneasy laugh, fumbling nervously with his pipe. The tension of the place had told on him as on Uchichak, and he felt irritated. "Nonsense; it's all moonshine, Montenay. That breed was simply scared stiff to remain with the Chipewas any longer, that's all. He was willing to join us, and to buy his safety with Noreen and some grub. Looked like a mighty good swap to me!"

Radison felt a most unreasonable desire to exculpate himself of some unknown offense, but Montenay only lay back and fell into his rambling, wheezing talk, staring up at the roof the while.

"Fourteen months ago it was, Jean Nichemus had trouble with an Eskimo over a narwhal-tooth knife. We was up north trading for ivory at the time—three weeks' trail from here. Three days after we left their village, Nichemus slipped out o' camp one night with his dogs. A week after we got back here without him he trailed into camp, half dead—but he had that knife, mind. Now, I say that a man like him don't give up a woman because a gang of Injuns look sideways at him—not much! What's more, I don't allow he's in bad with the Chipewas, for it don't stand to reason."

"Why not? After he failed in leading them against us, isn't it plausible that losing so many men would anger them?"

"Aye—it's plausible enough, man, which is just why I doubt it. If he'd come here with some cock-and-bull story, it might seem a good deal more convincing to my mind. No, friend Radisson; that snake wanted to find out if I was helpless, like Talking Owl prob'ly reported. There's why he came, if ye want to know—an' ye went an' told him I was bad off, eh?"

Radison nodded in silence. Montenay uttered a choking cough, spat blood, and hauled himself to a sitting position.

"Why? That's what I want to know, Radisson. Macferris Montenay don't pass out with two blows from a dog of a priest—not him! The breed is scared cold, but he's feared o' me—not o' Talking Owl, mind. The Chipewas have to stand by me to save their own necks, and they know it; so what's the breed's game? What in damnation is he after?"

The giant fairly roared out the last words and fell back gasping as the iron will loosened its grip on the broken body. Barr stared at him a moment, thoroughly alarmed; then turned to Macklin.

"What about it, Tom? Think Montenay is right?"

"I'm afraid so, old man. The more I think it over the fishier it looks, but unless he wants to supplant Montenay I can't see his object."

"Don't ye worry—he has one!" wheezed Montenay, his finger's closing and unclosing on the skins as he lay. "Moonshine, ye say, Radisson? Tut, tut—there's no moonshine in the brain o' Jean Nichemus! And Noreen's there—God!"

The giant gripped out at the skins, groaned once with agony, and sat up, choking. As Radison watched, astounded, a look of terrible earnestness swept across the shattered face of Montenay, he lurched forward, and with a convulsive effort that sent a trickle of crimson from his gasping mouth, actually gained his feet, staggering and swaying as he stood, but upborne by his dominant purpose.

"Radisson!" His voice was vibrant once more as of old, and brought Barr to his feet. "Radisson! As ye love her, man, undo the harm ye have done or I'll live to tear the throat out of ye yet!"

He caught wildly at the wall for support, and Barr reached forward to help him; but the giant shook him off, straightened up, and broke out in a cry of sheer agony.

"Helpless—helpless! An' that devil knows it—ah, quick! Take me to the village, Radisson—for God's sake don't delay, man! Ye don't know what devilment he's up to, an' there's a chance—ah!"

He pitched forward without warning and lay still. Barr uttered a stifled cry of horror, ran to his side, and turned him over. Raising his head with skins to relieve the unconscious man of the choking blood, the American lifted a haggard, ghastly face to Macklin.

"Tom, I believe he's right—but what can I do? We daren't leave this place before the Crees come. Uchichak's life wouldn't be worth a cent in the village, and, besides, we mustn't let the Chipewas knew that the Crees are following."

"The Crees may be lost," returned Macklin gloomily. "Sulvent may be dead by this time, Rad. It looks pretty black all around. When did Nichemus say he'd come with the girl?"

"To-morrow morning early."

"H-m! Can't see what he's got up his sleeve. He might have told the truth for a change, Barr. Still, Montenay's fearfully worked up about it, and that sure gets me going. He knows these guys better than we do, old scout! See here, Barr, I'm sick of this place. Think you could carry me out to the entrance? We could build a little fire there, and there are lots o' pelts."

"Sing out if I hurt you," returned Barr curtly, and stooped, gathering the furs about the injured Canadian. He realized how the last week had served to sap his strength when he raised Macklin and bore him to the entrance, and the muscles were standing out on his neck with the strain when finally he deposited the other at the side of Uchichak.

A cry of delight broke from Take-a-chance at sight of the dim twilight of the deep gorge, and he drew long breaths in keen enjoyment. The Cree was sitting staring out at the Chipewa watchman in the mouth of the pass, and something in his attitude reminded Radison of the sullen fury of a trapped animal waiting for the trapper. That terrible cavern had decidedly bad effects on all who entered it, concluded the American, but with grim scorn of it he left the two men at the entrance and returned to sleep beside Montenay.

He woke up to find the giant shaking him feebly with the one hand he could use, and at the muttered request for water Radison helped the other to sit up and drink. Montenay gasped and sank back, but his hand gripped that of Barr and held it.

"Radisson—what have ye done?"

"There's nothing to do, Montenay," returned the American hopelessly. "We'll have to wait and see what happens, I suppose."

"Wake up, man—don't sit there like a drunken man while Noreen may be in the arms of that devil at this minute! Wake up!"

The fierce, passion-filled words stirred a flame of dull rage in Radison, and he closed hard on Montenay's rough fingers for an instant.

"Tell me what to do, and by all that's holy I'll do it!"

"Do ye mean that, man?" rang the deep voice joyfully. "Then take me back to the village—I'll walk on your arm, Radisson—"

Barr's hard sense came back to him at the words.

"I couldn't give you freedom, for you know too much about Sulvent and the Crees."

"I'll say no word o' that! Talkin' Owl promised you peace—act, ye blasted fool! For the love o' that woman yonder, Radisson—save her from the breed! I'll give her to ye—I'll say nothin'—I'll do anything in God's world ye ask if ye'll but act, man! Keep her from the hands o' that smooth-tongued, black-souled devil—Radisson! Radisson! Are ye made o' stone? Act—*act!*"

Montenay's voice rose to a shriek, and he pulled himself up by Radison's hand. Barr's control gave way, and he reached for his rifle.

"Come!" he said hoarsely, catching Montenay's arm.

Lurching, but carried on by the awful earnestness of his fear, Montenay obeyed, and the two men slowly gained the cave-mouth. It was evening nominally, and Macklin awoke with a start, while Uchichak sprang up with ready knife at sight of the king.

"Stay here," commanded Barr curtly. "Mack, I'm taking Montenay to the village to see about this. The Crane will take care of you, and we may be back if we find all well."

Uchichak hesitated, then shot the knife home in its sheath.

"Strong Eyes is a man. *Miwasin!*" That guttural "Good!" was the last word that Barr ever heard from the Crane. A silent hand-clasp from Macklin, and he aided the gasping Montenay down the rock incline. At sight of their leader one shrill yell went up from the entrance to the gorge.

"Come along—we'll be there in a minute," grunted Barr. "Don't be afraid to rest on me, Montenay."

As they slowly neared the opening of the pass one man

advanced to meet them, and the American recognized Talking Owl.

"Whatcheer! Whatcheer!" uttered the chief gravely, but Montenay stopped.

"Nichemus—where is he? Quick, man!"

"At de village," came the reply, and the giant groaned, but pushed forward with new eagerness. Reaching the opening, a dozen Chipewas crowded around, Talking Owl gave a sharp order, and a dog-sled was brought up. Two men seized the traces while Montenay sank down on it, another slipped off his snow-shoes and handed them to Radison, and as if by some tacit understanding the little party drew down the slopes toward the village, which lay among the trees with slow smoke curling up from the lodges.

At the yell of Talking Owl men and squaws swarmed out to meet them, but Montenay lay with his great head sunk on his breast. Radison saw no trace of Nichemus among the advancing crowd, and urged on the two men who drew the sled, sharp anxiety in his heart. He could stand the suspense no longer, and with a word to the chief he plunged ahead of the sled through the Chipewas, who scattered at his approach.

He could see the shack that Noreen had occupied, but no smoke curled up from the mud-plastered chimney, and as he drew near he gave a shout. No sign of life appeared, no answer came, and with a sinking heart he dashed up to the door. It swung inward freely at his blow, and after one look the American staggered back with a hoarse cry. Montenay's forebodings had been fulfilled—Noreen was gone.

CHAPTER XIX

PURSUIT

"CALM YOURSELF, man! Calm yourself—give me a chance to find out something!"

Curiously enough, it was the raging whirlwind of a Montenay who was now quiet and self-possessed, while the ordinarily cool but high-strung American was madly raving at the Chipewas and the absent breed. The steady voice of the giant calmed him, and Montenay, beckoning to some of the warriors who had remained at the village, exchanged a few crisp sentences in Chipewa, then nodded slowly and painfully.

"As I thought, Radisson, Nichemus came straight back and loaded up a sled, then went off to the west, right after his talk with you. He told the braves it was by my orders, but it's easy enough to guess what he told Noreen."

Barr groaned, remembering the ring and the foxskin letter. The flame of rage that had raged within him suddenly died down to a cold, merciless fury, and he pointed with his rifle.

"Get me dogs and some grub, Montenay—but where on earth could he go?"

"Straight west," returned Montenay grimly. "He prob'ly figures on circling the hills and heading back to the post. He took my dogs, what's more."

"Well, get me some huskies and a load of grub!" exclaimed Barr impatiently. The ghost of a smile flickered over that beplastered face.

"Quietly, man! Give us your hand."

Radison aided Montenay in getting to his feet, and by some sixth sense he felt the iron determination of the man reach out and master him. The giant coughed blood for a long minute, then spat out orders right and left in Chipewa. Instantly the men sprang to action.

While Talking Owl visited the lodges, snake-whip in hand,

and selected six of the best dogs in the village, other warriors
loaded down the sled with pemmican bricks, frozen whitefish,
and other necessary supplies. Before the dogs were beaten into
the harness a heavy bearskin robe was fetched, and Montenay
painfully wrapped himself in it; then he was placed on the sled
and lashed in place.

"Montenay! You're never going to try to make the trip?" cried
Radison anxiously. "Why, you're crazy to think of it, man!"

"Then I'm crazed in a good cause, Barr. Aye, I'm going. Think
you I could stay here while that devil carries Noreen off into
the hills? Broken man I may be, but the Lord help Jean Nichemus when I lay hands on him, for nothing else will!"

Grimly Radison echoed the thought, making no further
protest as the sled was prepared. Disabled though the giant was,
he was by no means sorry to have his company, for Montenay
must know the country like a book. Besides, the very manner
of the man, quiet and collected as it was, thrilled with an un-
derlying savagery that boded ill for Nichemus when they found
the breed.

"And we'll find him," vowed the American, gripping his rifle.
"And if he's darned to lay a finger on Noreen—"

The thought was cut short by the sharp crack of a whip, for
Montenay could use one arm, though the effort cost him untold
anguish. The idea of taking Talking Owl with them crossed his
mind, but he dismissed it instantly. The chase might be a long
one, and the food supply on the sled was none too large for the
two of them.

"Mash! Mash!"

Circling ahead, a number of the Chipewas had already
located the trail of Nichemus, and Radison swung into it with
a rush, intent only upon covering ground as fast as he could,
and with that object he struck a terrific pace that soon left the
village behind. Something about the trail impressed him with
a dim sense of familiarity, and, looking around, he found that
Nichemus had run in toward the cliffs, much as he himself had

done when escaping with Noreen. Evidently the breed was making for that same break in the line of cliffs, he thought.

As he ran he saw that they were passing that inner snow-line formed by the broken sections of the crags, and his thoughts flew back to that desperate battle under the lights, when Sulvent had saved them—but where was Sulvent now?

"The Crees couldn't have been delayed all this time, surely," he reflected. "Either the *père* got lost or else—oh, Lord, there's no use speculating!"

With which he gave himself wholly up to the business in hand. In one respect he had a tremendous advantage over the fugitive, for Nichemus had been forced to break new trail, that made by Barr and Noreen having been snowed under, while Radison was plodding along in the packed snow without effort. This would in large measure discount the start gained by Nichemus, who had no doubt planned that Radison would not grow suspicious until the next morning. With that start he would have stood a good chance of getting clear, but now the pursuers had a fighting chance at least.

Suddenly it occurred to Barr that, since it was easier to follow than to lead and with the trail already broken, he could drive the dogs ahead of him and attain even more speed, perhaps. He stopped and turned aside, but as the sled drew past he saw that Montenay lay back, blood frozen on his hood and the whip dragging listlessly from its thong.

"Poor devil!" thought the American, gently taking the whip from the hanging mitten. "I'll just let him lie. His exertions back there were too much for him—he must be driving ahead on his will-power alone. *Mash*, there, *mash!*"

The dogs held the trail steadily enough, but Barr forced them relentlessly forward at a racing pace. A little spume-cloud was stirred up from the frost-bitten snow, driving back from the dogs and sled, and the dragging snowshoe-heels sent up another, so that the American was soon striding along like the white "ghost" of Père Sulvent, while overhead the Spirit Dancers took the stage amid the usual faint hissing rumble from the horizon.

After three hours he perceived that the terrific spurt was working havoc with the dogs, but he held on until he came to a bare spot beneath the cliffs where Nichemus had made camp—the ashes of his fire not yet quite cold. Here he found evidence of the desperate haste with which the breed had fled, for near the fire lay the body of a dog, shot through the head, its frozen tongue lolling far out of its mouth.

"Askwa!"

At his shout the dogs dropped where they stood, only too glad to rest. Swiftly Radison collected birch-bark and got a blaze flaring, and when he had melted some snow and forced the water into Montenay's mouth, the giant was able to eat— somewhat gingerly, for Sulvent's iron fist had not spared his teeth. Montenay spoke only once, when he saw the body of the dead dog.

"Good! He has one huskie the less, and we're sure of him now, Radisson! When we get him I'm going to rip the hide off him with a dog-whip, first."

Unobtrusively but anxiously Radison watched him. Montenay was plainly in bad shape, and he doubted if the giant could last much longer. Before they started there came a coughing spell, and the American saw that only by a great effort did Montenay fight off the faintness again. He managed to load himself aboard the sled, but after Barr had started he looked down to find the other lying unconscious once more.

"We'll have rough going once we get into the hills," and the American gazed ahead at the break in the line of cliffs which he knew so well. "Nichemus seems to be following my—Hello! *Askwa!*"

The dogs stopped obediently and Barr caught up his rifle from the sled, where it lay at Montenay's feet. Among the trees to the right he had caught a glimpse of moving figures, and as he stopped the dogs these darted out over the snow. A cry of amazed relief broke from Radison as he recognized the tall, gaunt figure of Père Sulvent in the lead, and, flinging down his rifle, he swept out to meet them.

"Radison, as I'm a sinner!" ejaculated the no less astonished priest, their hands gripping. "What are you doing here, of all places? What's that on the sled?"

A score of silent men followed Sulvent, and behind them were others with dog-sleds. Barr woke to action, realizing that he was losing time.

"Quick—give me fresh dogs—I'm after Nichemus! He has stolen Noreen, but I'm gaining on him—"

Sulvent waited to hear no more. Turning, he issued a rapid-fire of orders to his men, and the Crees hastened up with the sleds. One of these was dumped clear of its load, six of the best dogs were selected from the other trains, and rifles and were lashed to the sled. Recalling Montenay, Barr prang to the side of Sulvent.

"I've got Montenay on that sled! He's in a bad way—unconscious, but he insisted on coming with me. Let your men take him back. You'll find Macklin in the—"

"I'll be finding Noreen first," returned the other grimly, and Radison thrilled with fresh vigor. The battle was as good as won, he felt, with this man of iron at his side!

Issuing orders to Pekoos, or the Sandfly, who was in charge of the party, to take every care of Montenay and not to attack the Chipewas, Sulvent wasted no time asking questions, but his long lash sent the huskies leaping into the trail. Uchichak's son waved them farewell and they were off.

As they ran behind the sled the two men outlined their stories. After telling of what had happened at the cave, Radison learned that Sulvent had met the Crees safely and had led them around through the hills, in order to fall on the village from behind. Pekoos and his men had been terrified by that fearsome gorge, but when they were assured that Sulvent was no ghost they had eagerly placed themselves under his leadership.

Now began a journey such as the American had never dreamed of and hoped never to experience again. While trailing with Macklin he had thought the Canadian a hard worker, but Père Sulvent was tenfold harder. There was something dour and purposeful in his very face, something that emanated from him and filled Barr with savage determination to keep up till he dropped in his tracks.

And he needed all his energy, for Sulvent kept up the race until the whimpering dogs fell from sheer exhaustion, but the man seemed tireless. They halted for two smokes in order to let the dogs recover, then plunged forward again, the lonely Ghost Hills all around them and only that faint track in the snow to lead them aright.

"He knows the road right enough," declared the priest. "So the dog swore on the *bon Dieu* that he would obey Montenay—and then broke the oath, did he? Wait, Jean Nichemus! 'Tis a bad day for you when you get Michael Sulvent oh your trail, no less! He'll be thinking I'm a ghost, of course, but I'll soon show him otherwise!"

Barr wondered that the breed made no effort to disguise his trail, but Sulvent scoffed at the idea of hiding a dog-train's track in the hills. If it had been the open country, with ice-covered lake and rivers to fling off the scent by, it would be another matter; but here the pursuit would be close and deadly, and the only hope of Nichemus was in the speed of his dogs.

With eager exultation Radison found that this sole hope was failing the breed, for they passed another stopping-place in a valley, and after feeling the ashes of the fire left there, Sulvent declared confidently that another three or four hours would tiring them up to their quarry. Glancing at the tall form of the priest, clad in the bearskin that Montenay had formerly worn, Barr chuckled in spite of his weariness; there would be a double-barreled surprise for Nichemus before long!

They encountered no bare spots such as had caused Barr so much trouble in his former flight, for the breed seemed to pick his way cunningly. Sulvent halted the dogs as they wound down a long valley and seized one of the rifles.

"Take the other gun, Radison. I know a trick worth two of this. We'll cut over the hill and be on top of the divil in an hour, for I'm certain of the way now."

Barr obeyed without a protest, too exhausted to talk. Leaving the dogs and sled huddled up in the snow together, Sulvent led him over a bleak ridge of naked rock, their snow-shoes on their backs. Down the next valley they went, and after another climb that left the American wind-spent and aching, they gained a crest and the priest halted.

"Ah—look!"

New life leaped into Radison at sight of a black speck far down the valley, and now he swept along after Sulvent with a grim thirst for vengeance goading him forward and making him forget his aching limb; and the pain that throbbed in his throat as he gasped the frosty air into his lungs.

For a while they lost sight of the fugitive, but from the trail could see that Nichemus was no longer breaking trail ahead of the sled, but had taken the traces and was helping the dogs forward, warned perhaps by some subtle sense of danger that his every effort was needed. Then the valley made a sharp curve, and as they swept around it Barr got sight of the quarry not a half-mile ahead.

Sulvent set a terrible pace now, taking Radison to the utmost to keep up; but he locked his teeth and held to it, for they were gaining fast.

That they were seen became evident, for suddenly Nichemus stopped as he ran, and a black dot fell away. When they reached it Barr found that it was one of the dogs slashed free—panting, unable to move.

The other dogs must have given out almost at the same time, for they saw Nichemus swing back to the sled, seize the rifle, and dart behind a clump of small jack-pine.

Down upon him they rushed, with no thought for danger,

and Radison uncased his rifle while he ran. The trees spurted red flame, and a bullet sang overhead droningly. Barr answered it with a volley, but knew that his bullets must have gone wild. Now they were but three hundred yards distant—two hundred—one hundred—and the breed had reserved his fire.

With not fifty yards between him and the sled, on which he could make out the figure of Noreen, Barr suddenly saw two quick spats of flame among the trees. At the same instant Père Sulvent flung the hood from his gaunt head, but too late.

The American felt a shock; something bit and ripped into his body, and with a vain effort to keep his shoes from tripping him he went forward and plowed head first into the snow.

CHAPTER XX

TRAIL'S END

THE SHAPES moved slowly across the snow—first a tall, gaunt figure in heavy bearskin capote, and after him two sleds drawn by weary, dragging dogs.

On the first sled lay a motionless body, which might have been thought lifeless but for the faint jets of rime from the hood which bespoke slow breathing.

On the second sat a girl whose violet eyes rested ever on the sled ahead.

There was a low wailing from closed lodges as Pekoos, at the head of a score of Crees, left the village to meet the arrivals; but the aspect of the Crees was not that of conquerors. There were no yells of exultation, no *feu-de-joie* from muskets and rifles, but the warriors moved with slow tread, and the face of the Sandfly was set and cold, though none of his men bore traces of conflict.

Reaching the Crees, Sulvent exchanged a single "Whatcheer!" with the young chief, who thereupon fell into step beside him and said no more. The priest sent a sharp glance at that inscrutable brown face, but knew better than to ask questions.

Something had happened, and what it was would come out when the Sandfly was ready to speak, and not before. More than one Cree cast a glance of fear at the silent priest.

As they wound between the lodges one or two Chipewa squaws peered out and hastily closed the caribou-hide flaps again, but the keen wails of lamentation never ceased to rise.

Macklin, looking rather pale and shaken, lay on some skins near a fire before the large shack of Montenay. As the party came up he rose on one elbow and held out a mittened hand, with a faint smile on his raw-boned face.

"Hello, father! But—where's Radison—and Nichemus?"

Sulvent gripped the hand for a moment, but did not reply. At a sharp order in Cree a number of warriors took Barr from the sled and bore him inside the shack. Unheeding Macklin's startled exclamation, Sulvent turned to Noreen, who had come up.

"Noreen, my dear, this is Tom Macklin, as true-hearted a man as ever wore moccasin."

She took the Canadian's hand with a smile.

"I've heard a good deal about you from Père Sulvent," she said simply, "and—and I want to thank you for all you've done to help me!"

"Shucks! Don't thank me—thank the father here and Rad, Miss Murphy! Tell me, is he hurt?" he added anxiously.

"A little. We must get the bullet out right away."

"We? H-m! I guess I understand why Barr—"

"Come, Noreen," broke in Sulvent abruptly. " 'Tis a stiff job we have, and no nice one, and so the quicker done the better. Stay here, Macklin—we'll be having a talk later."

Ordering the Crees to build a roaring fire in the shack, Sulvent entered with Noreen, while Macklin stared after them with anxious eyes. The priest bent over Radison, who lay on the rude couch, and opened the capote.

"Still feverish he is. Now, Noreen, will you be getting some water and a bandage? No; keep away till I've done. Pekoos!"

The young chief took Radison's arm, holding the American firmly but gently while Sulvent laid bare the wound and drew out his knife. With untrembling hand the priest cut deep, Barr groaned—and it was over.

As Sulvent picked out the bullet Noreen went to her knees and bandaged the shoulder deftly. Five minutes later, her lips ashen, she sat beside Macklin while the priest told his story.

"Afther Radison went down I went for Nichemus. He saw the face o' me, took me for a ghost, and tried to run, but fell over his dogs, and when I got to him I found his own knife in his heart.

"Barr was bad hit in the shoulder, but I thought the bullet might work out, not daring to cut down, for fear o' the frost-bite. So we hitched up and came in—and now, praise be, the lad's promising to do well. Where's Montenay and the Crane?"

Macklin waved a hand toward the black notch in the hills above.

"A few hours after Rad and Montenay left, father, Talking Owl came to the cave. He said that Montenay had ordered him to spare my life, and his young men were eager to attack Uchichak. Of course, I said I'd take a chance on staying with the Crane, but he reached over and took my gun, then told Talking Owl to send after me.

"What happened after that I'm a little mixed on—like every one else, I guess. While the Chipewas were coming for me I saw the Crane carry out some of those little kegs of powder; then he shook hands with me, and the Chipewas carried me down here. I saw Talking Owl lead his men for the cave on the jump, but Uchichak had two rifles and an automatic to hold them off with, and he did it for half an hour. Then your Crees swept into the village, and they were just starting for the gorge up there when there came an explosion that must have been the powder-kegs. Maybe Uchichak tried to work our stunt with loose powder and fooled himself—I don't know. Anyhow, some of the Chipewas came back and bumped into the Crees, and there was a bit of a mix-up!"

"And Montenay?"

"He was lying beside me here, watching things, and just managed to get on his feet to mix in the scrap when a wild bullet hit him."

For a moment Sulvent lifted his iron face to the sky, fingering the crucifix at his neck.

"*De mortuis nil nisi bonum.* He was a brave man, rest his soul!"

The fourth day after reaching camp Barr Radison sat at the shack doorway talking with Macklin. Those who were left at the Chipewas had come in on promise of peace, but Talking Owl and a good share of his warriors lay in the narrow gorge with Uchichak, buried under tons of rock.

The powder must have been set off in the very mouth of the cave, for the whole front of the cliff was blown down. But the grief of the Crees was tempered by pride in their dead chief when they had learned the manner of his end.

"And that finishes off the black-fox pelts," puffed Macklin reflectively. "Well, it's better so for the market—though I'd have liked to see McShayne when we brought 'em in! Reckon these Ghost Hills will have enough to haunt 'em for quite a spell now, Rad! Well, how do you feel?"

"It's a bit sore, but after—"

"Oh, shucks, I don't mean that! Inside, I mean! Still feel as though you'd wasted the last six years?"

"I guess not, Tom," grinned Radison. "As I said back there in the cave, I've got my grip again—things seem just about right as they are. Lord, I'll be glad to get out of this place, though! Yes, I'm glad I'm just where I am, all around."

"You ought to be," grunted the other. "She's only three years younger than you, at that!"

A soft crunch of snow sounded at their side, and as Macklin

looked up he caught the laughing eyes of Noreen fixed on him, and his brick-red face turned scarlet.

"Excuse me," and he leaped up—"I got to see to some meat I left over the fire!"

Barr gazed after him, smiling, and Noreen sat at his side looking up at the crags which stretched to right and left.

"We leave in three days for the post, Barr. Père Sulvent just told me. Are you glad?"

"If there weren't a dozen Crees out there I'd show you just how glad I am, dear!" His dancing eyes gripped hers for a moment. "We aren't going back through the pass?"

"No—the other way. The good father will take us through the hills when the hunters get back. You'll have to go by sled, for the first week, anyway. Then, if you're very good, we'll let you take to the shoes slowly."

"Much obliged," laughed the American. His face sobered as he gazed down at her. "It'll be a long trip, Noreen, but this time we'll weather through safely, and—"

"And?" she repeated, looking up at his rugged features with a little smile.

"And there'll be all of life at the trail's end, dear," he said softly as his hand closed over hers.

H. BEDFORD-JONES

BEDFORD-JONES IS a Canadian by birth, but not by profession, having removed to the United States at the age of one year. For over twenty years he has been more or less profitably engaged in writing and traveling. As he has seldom resided in one place longer than a year or so and is a person of retiring habits, he is somewhat a man of mystery; more than once he has suffered from unscrupulous gentlemen who impersonated him—one of whom murdered a wife and was subsequently shot by the police, luckily after losing his alias.

The real Bedford-Jones is an elderly man, whose gray hair and precise attire give him rather the appearance of a retired foreign diplomat. His hobby is stamp collecting, and his collection of Japan is said to be one of the finest in existence. At present writing he is en route to Morocco, and when this appears in print he will probably be somewhere on the Mojave Desert in company with Erle Stanley Gardner.

Questioned as to the main facts in his life, he declared there was only one main fact, but it was not for publication; that his life had been uneventful except for numerous financial losses, and that his only adventures lay in evading adventurers. In his younger years he was something of an athlete, but the encroachments of age preclude any active pursuits except that of motoring. He is usually to be found poring over his stamps, working at his typewriter, or laboring in his California rose garden, which is one of the sights of Cathedral Cañon, near Palm Springs.

Bedford-Jones has written stories laid in many corners of the earth, but among his most popular tales were the John Solomon stories which started many years ago in the *Argosy*.

www.ingramcontent.com/pod-product-compliance
Lightning Source LLC
Chambersburg PA
CBHW070932250626
47159CB00009B/3216